"A few hours till dinner? You must be home earlier than usual then."

She meant for the comment to be teasing. Evidently, Grant wasn't the workaholic she'd assumed he was if he ended his office hours early enough to have some relaxation time before dinner. The realization heartened her. Maybe he did have something in common with his twin.

But Grant didn't take the comment as teasing. "Yeah, I am, actually," he said matter-of-factly. "But there wasn't anything at the office I couldn't bring home with me, and I thought maybe you—and Hank, too, for that matter—I thought both of you, actually, might... um..."

Somehow, she knew he'd intended to end the sentence with the words *need me*, but decided at the last minute to say something else instead. Something else that clearly hadn't yet formed in his brain, though, because no other words came out of his mouth to help the thought along.

But Clara had trouble figuring out what to say next, too, mostly because she was too busy drowning in the deep blue depths of Grant's eyes to be able to recognize much of anything else.

* * *

A CEO in Her Stocking is part of the Accidental Heirs duet: First they find their fortunes, then they find love

Dear Reader,

Christmas is, hands down, my favorite holiday and has been since I was a kid. The only thing that could have ever made it more fun would have been to have someone show up at my door and say, “Merry Christmas! You’re the long-lost heir to a Park Avenue fortune!” Which is exactly what happens to Clara Easton in *A CEO in Her Stocking*.

Well, okay, maybe that’s not *exactly* what happens, since it’s actually her three-year-old son who’s inherited the fortune. But Clara finds her life turned upside down by his windfall. Especially when she meets little Hank’s Park Avenue CEO uncle, Grant Dunbarton. He may look exactly like Hank’s late father, but that’s where the similarities end. And he seems to have completely lost sight of what Christmas is all about. There’s little comfort or joy to be had where he’s concerned, and he’s not exactly a jolly, happy soul. Good thing Clara and Hank are there to deck his halls and bring a little joy to his world. Now if he’ll just let his heart prepare them room.

Okay, enough with the carols. I do hope you enjoy getting to know Clara and Grant as much as I did. And I hope your holidays are merry and bright!

Cheers!

Elizabeth Bevarly

A CEO IN HER STOCKING

ELIZABETH BEVARLY

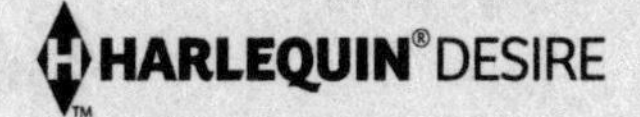

Recycling programs for this product may not exist in your area.

ISBN-13: 978-0-373-73425-2

A CEO in Her Stocking

Reclaimed by the Rancher

The publisher acknowledges Janice Maynard for her contribution to *Reclaimed by the Rancher*.

This edition published by arrangement with Harlequin Books S.A.

For questions and comments about the quality of this book, please contact us at CustomerService@Harlequin.com.

Printed in U.S.A.

HARLEQUIN®
www.Harlequin.com

CONTENTS

A CEO IN HER STOCKING 7
Elizabeth Bevarly

RECLAIMED BY THE RANCHER 187
Janice Maynard

Elizabeth Bevarly is a *New York Times* bestselling and award-winning author of more than seventy novels and novellas. Her books have been translated into two dozen languages and published in three dozen countries, and she hopes to someday be as well traveled herself. An honors graduate of the University of Louisville, she has called home places as diverse as San Juan, Puerto Rico, and Haddonfield, New Jersey, but now writes full-time in her native Kentucky, usually on a futon between two cats. She loves reading, movies, British and Canadian TV shows, and fiddling with soup recipes. Visit her on the web at elizabethbevarly.com, follow her on Twitter or send her a friend request on Facebook.

Books by Elizabeth Bevarly

HARLEQUIN DESIRE

Taming the Prince
Taming the Beastly M.D.
Married to His Business
The Billionaire Gets His Way

The Accidental Heirs

Only on His Terms
A CEO in Her Stocking

Visit the Author Profile page at Harlequin.com, or elizabethbevarly.com, for more titles.

A CEO IN HER STOCKING

Elizabeth Bevarly

For David and Eli,
the people who made Christmas
even better than it already was.

Prologue

Clara Easton was dabbing one final icing berry onto a poinsettia cupcake when the bell over the entrance to Tybee Island's Bread & Buttercream rang for what she hoped was the last time that day. Not that she wasn't grateful for every customer, but with Thanksgiving just over and Christmas barely a month away, the bakery had been getting hammered. Not to mention she had to pick up Hank from his sitter in... She glanced at the clock. Yikes! Thirty minutes! Where had the day gone?

With luck, the customer was someone who'd just remembered she needed a dessert for a weekend party, and *Hey, whatever you have left in the case is fine—I'll take it.* But the visitor was neither a she nor a customer, Tilly, the salesclerk, told Clara when she came back to the kitchen. It was a man asking for her as *Miss Easton.* A man in a suit. Carrying a briefcase.

Which was kind of weird, since no one on the island

called her anything but Clara, and few if any of her customers were business types—or men, for that matter. Moms and brides pretty much kept Bread & Buttercream in business. Clara was intrigued enough that she didn't take time to remove her apron before heading into the shop. She did at least tuck a few raven curls under the white kerchief tied on her head pirate-style.

Though the man might have fit right in on the island with his surfer dude good looks, he clearly wasn't local. His suit was too well cut, his hair too well styled, and he looked completely out of his element amid the white wrought-iron café sets and murals of cartoon cupcakes.

"Hi," Clara greeted him. "Can I help you?"

"Miss Easton?" he asked.

"Clara," she automatically corrected him. *Miss Easton* sounded like a Victorian spinster who ran a boardinghouse for young ladies required to be home by nine o'clock in order to preserve their reputations and their chastity.

"Miss Easton," the man repeated anyway. "My name is August Fiver. I work for Tarrant, Fiver and Twigg. Attorneys."

He extended a business card that bore his name and title—Senior Vice-President and Probate Researcher—and an address in New York City. Clara knew probate had something to do with wills, but she didn't know anyone who had died. She had no family except for her son, and all of her friends were fine.

"Probate researcher?" she asked.

He nodded. "My firm is hired to find heirs who are, for lack of a better term, long-lost relatives of…certain estates."

The explanation did nothing to clear things up. From what Clara knew about the two people who had exchanged enough bodily fluids to produce her, whatever they might have for her to inherit was either stolen or conned. She would just as soon have them stay long lost.

Her confusion must have shown on her face, because August Fiver told her, "It's your son, Henry. I'm here on behalf of his paternal grandmother, Francesca Dunbarton." His lips turned up in just the hint of a smile as he added, "Of the Park Avenue Dunbartons."

Clara's mouth dropped open. She'd spent almost a month with Hank's father four summers ago, when she was working the counter of Bread & Buttercream. Brent had been charming, funny and sweet, with the eyes of a poet, the mouth of a god and a body that could have been roped off in an Italian museum. He'd lived in a tent, played the guitar and read aloud to her by firelight. Then, one morning, he was gone, moving on to whatever came next in his life.

Clara hadn't really minded that much. She hadn't loved him, and she'd had plans for her future that didn't include him. They deliberately hadn't exchanged last names, so certain had both been that whatever they had was temporary. They'd had fun for a few weeks, but like all good things, it had come to an end.

Except it didn't quite come to an end. When Clara discovered she was pregnant, she felt obliged to contact Brent and let him know—she'd still had his number in her phone. But her texts to him about her condition went unanswered, as did her messages when she tried to call. Then the number was disconnected. It hadn't been easy raising a child alone. It still wasn't. But Clara managed. It was her and Hank against the world. And that was just fine with her.

"I didn't realize Brent came from money," she said. "He wasn't… We weren't… That summer was…" She gave up trying to describe what defied description. "I'm surprised he even told his mother about Hank. I'm sorry Mrs. Dunbarton passed away without meeting her grandson."

At this, August Fiver's expression sobered. "Mrs. Dunbarton is alive and well. I'm afraid it's Brent who's passed away."

For the second time in as many minutes, Clara was struck dumb. She tried to identify how she felt about the news of Brent's death and was distressed to discover she had no idea how to feel. It had just been so long since she'd seen him.

"As your son is Brent Dunbarton's sole heir, everything that belonged to him now belongs to Henry. A not insignificant sum."

Not insignificant, Clara echoed to herself. What did that mean?

"One hundred and forty-two million," August Fiver said.

Her stomach dropped. Surely she heard that wrong. He must mean one hundred and forty-two million Legos. Or action figures. Or Thomas the Tank Engines. Those things did seem to multiply quickly. Surely he didn't mean one hundred and forty-two million—

"Dollars," he said, clearing that up. "Mr. Dunbarton's estate—your son's inheritance—is worth in excess of one hundred and forty-two million dollars. And your son's grandmother is looking forward to meeting you both. So is Brent's brother, Grant. I've been charged by them with bringing you and Henry to New York as soon as possible. Can you be ready to leave tomorrow?"

One

Clara had never traveled north of Knoxville, Tennessee. Everything she knew about New York City she'd learned from television and movies, none of which had prepared her for the reality of buildings dissolving into the sky and streets crammed with people and taxis. Even so, as the big town car carrying her, Hank and Gus—as August Fiver had instructed her to call him—turned onto Park Avenue, Clara was beginning to get an inkling about why New York was a town so nice they named it twice.

Ultimately, it had taken four days to leave Tybee Island. Packing for a toddler took a day in itself, and Clara had orders that weekend for a birthday party, a baby shower, a bunco night and a wedding cake. Then there were all the arrangements she needed to make with Hank's preschool and covering shifts at Bread & Buttercream. Thank goodness the week after Thanksgiving was slow enough, barely, to manage that before the Christmas season lurched into gear.

Looking out the window now, she could scarcely believe her eyes. The city was just...awesome. She hated to use such a trite word for such a spectacular place, but she couldn't think of anything more fitting.

"Mama, this is *awesome*!"

Clara smiled at her son. Okay, maybe that was why she couldn't think of another word for it. Because *awesome* was about the only adjective you heard when you had a three-year-old.

Hank strained against the belt of the car seat fastened between her and Gus, struggling to get a glimpse at the passing urban landscape, his fascination as rabid as Clara's. That was where much of their alikeness ended, however. Although he had her black curls and green eyes, too, his face was a copy of Brent's. His disposition was also like his father's. He was easygoing and quick to laugh, endlessly curious about *every*thing and rarely serious.

But Clara was glad Hank was different from her in that respect. She'd been a serious little girl. Things like fun and play had been largely absent from her childhood, and she'd learned early on to never ask questions, because it would only annoy the grown-ups. Such was life for a ward of the state of Georgia, who was shuttled from foster home to children's home to group home and back again. It was why she was determined that her son's life would be as free from turbulence as she could make it, and why he would be well-rooted in one place. She just hoped this inheritance from Brent didn't mess with either of those things.

The car rolled to a halt before a building of a dozen stories whose stone exterior was festooned with gold wreaths for the holidays. Topiaries sparkling with white lights dotted the front walkway leading to beveled lattice windows and French doors, and a red-liveried doorman stood sentry at the front door. It was exactly the kind of place where people would live when they were the owners of an industrial empire that had been in their family for two centuries. The Dunbartons could trace their roots all the way back to England, Gus had told her, where they were distantly related to a duke. Meaning that Hank could potentially become king, if the Black Death returned and took out the several thousand people standing between him and the throne.

The building's lobby was as sumptuous as its exterior, all polished marble and gleaming mahogany bedecked with evergreen boughs and swaths of red velvet ribbon. And when they took the elevator to the top floor, the doors unfolded on more of the same, since the penthouse foyer was decorated with enough poinsettias to germinate a banana republic. Clara curled her arm around Hank's shoulders to hug him close, and Gus seemed to sense her anxiety. He smiled reassuringly as he rang the bell. She glanced at Hank to make sure he was presentable, and, inescapably, had to stoop to tie his sneaker.

"Mr. Fiver," she heard someone greet Gus in a crisp, formal voice.

Butler, she decided as she looped Hank's laces into a serviceable bow. And wow, was the man good at butlering. He totally sounded like someone who was being paid good money to be cool and detached.

"Mr. Dunbarton," Gus replied.

Oh. Okay. Not the butler. Brent's brother. She couldn't remember what Brent's voice had sounded like, but she was sure it hadn't been anywhere near as solemn.

Laces tied, Clara stood to greet their host, and… And took a small step backward, her breath catching in her chest. Because Hank's father had risen from the grave, looking as somber as death itself.

Or maybe not. On closer consideration, Clara saw little of Brent in his brother's blue eyes and close-cropped dark hair. Brent's eyes had laughed with merriment, and his hair had been long enough to dance in the ocean breeze. The salient cheekbones, trenchant jaw and elegant nose were the same, but none were burnished by the caress of salt and sun. And the mouth… Oh, the mouth. Brent's mouth had been perpetually curled into an irreverent smile, full and beautiful, the kind of mouth that incited a woman to commit mayhem. This version was flat and uncompromising, clearly not prone to smiles. And where Brent had worn nothing but T-shirts and baggy shorts, this man was dressed in charcoal trousers, a crisp white Oxford shirt, maroon necktie and black vest.

So it wasn't Zombie Brent. It was Brent's very much alive brother. Brent's very much alive *twin* brother. The mirror image of a man who had, one summer, filled Clara with a happiness unlike any she had ever known, and left her with the gift of a son who would ensure that happiness stayed with her forever.

A mirror image of that man who resembled him not at all.

She wasn't what he'd expected.

Then again, Grant Dunbarton wasn't sure exactly what he had expected the mother of Brent's son to be. His brother had been completely indiscriminate when it came to women. Brent had been indiscriminate about everything. Women, cars, clothes. Friends, family, society. Promises, obligations, responsibilities. You name it, it had held Brent's attention for as long as it interested him—which was rarely more than a few days. Then he'd moved on to something else. He'd been the poster child for Peter Pan Syndrome, no matter how old he was.

Actually, Grant reconsidered, there had been one way his brother discriminated when it came to women. All of them had been jaw-droppingly beautiful. Clara Easton was no exception. Her hair was a riot of black curls, her mouth was as plump and red as a ripe pepper and her eyes were a green so pale and so clear they seemed to go on forever. She was tall, too, probably pushing six feet in her spike-heeled boots.

She might have looked imperious, but she had her arm roped protectively around her son in a way that indicated she was clearly uncomfortable. Grant supposed that shouldn't be surprising. It wasn't every day that a woman who'd been spawned by felons and raised in a string of sketchy environments discovered she'd given birth to the equivalent of American royalty.

Because the Dunbartons of Park Avenue—formerly the Dunbartons of Rittenhouse Square and, before that, the Dunbartons of Beacon Hill—were a family whose name had, since Revolutionary times, been mentioned in the same breath with the Hancocks, Astors, Vanderbilts and Rockefellers. Still, Grant admired her effort to make herself look invulnerable. It was actually kind of cute.

And then there was the boy. He was going to be a problem. Except for his hair and eye color—both a contribution from his mother—he was a replica of his father at that age. Grant hoped his own mother didn't fall apart again when she saw Henry Easton. She'd been a mess since hearing the news of Brent's drowning off the coast of Sri Lanka in the spring. It had only been last month that she'd finally pulled herself together enough to go through his things. Then, when she came across the will none of them knew he'd made and discovered he had a child none of them knew he'd fathered, she'd broken down again.

This time, though, there had been joy tempering the grief. There was a remnant of Brent out there in the world somewhere. In Georgia, of all places. Grant had been worried they'd need a paternity test to ensure Henry Easton really was a Dunbarton before they risked dashing his mother's hopes. But the boy's undeniable resemblance to Brent—and to Grant, for that matter—made that unnecessary.

"Ms. Easton," he said as warmly as he could—though, admittedly, warmth wasn't his strong suit. Brent had pretty much sucked up all the affability genes in the Dunbarton DNA while they were still in the womb. Which was fine, because it left Grant with all the efficiency genes, and those carried a person a lot further in life. "It's nice to finally meet you. You, too," he told Henry.

"It's nice to meet you, too, Mr. Dunbarton," Clara said, her voice low and husky and as bewitching as the rest of her.

A Southern drawl tinted her words, something Grant would have thought he'd find disagreeable, but instead found…well, kind of hot.

She nudged her son lightly. "Right, Hank? Say hello to Mr. Dunbarton."

"Hello, Mr. Dunbarton," the boy echoed dutifully.

Grant did his best to smile. "You don't have to call me Mr. Dunbarton. You can call me…"

He started to say *Uncle Grant*, but the words got

stuck in his throat. *Uncle* wasn't a word that sat well with him. Uncles were affable, easygoing guys who told terrible jokes and pulled nickels from people's ears. Uncles wore argyle sweaters and brought six-packs to Thanksgiving dinner. Uncles taught their nephews the things fathers wouldn't, like where to hide their *Playboys* and how to get fake IDs. No way was Grant suited to the role of uncle.

So he said, "Call me Grant." When he looked at Clara Easton again, he added, "You, too."

"Thank you…Grant," she said. Awkwardly. In her Southern accent. That was kind of hot.

She glanced at her son. But Henry remained silent, only gazing at Grant with his mother's startlingly green eyes.

"Come in," he said to all of them.

August Fiver did, but Clara hesitated, clearly not confident of their reception, her arm still draped around her son's shoulder.

"Please," Grant tried again, extending his hand toward the interior. "You are welcome here."

Clara still didn't look convinced, but the intrepid Henry took an experimental step forward, his gaze never leaving Grant's. Then he took a second, slightly larger, step. Then a third, something that pulled him free of his mother's grasp. She looked as if she wanted to yank him back, but remained rooted where she stood.

"My mother is looking forward to meeting you," Grant said, hoping the mention of another woman might make her feel better. But mention of his mother only made her look more panicked.

"Is something wrong, Ms. Easton?"

By now, Henry had followed Fiver through the door, so the three of them looked expectantly at Clara. She glanced first at her son, then at Grant. For a moment, he honestly thought she would grab her son and bolt. Then, finally, she strode forward. Again, Grant was impressed by her attempt to seem more confident than she was. This time, though, it didn't seem cute. This time, it seemed kind of…

Hmm. That was weird. For a minute there, he felt toward Clara the way she must have felt when she roped her arm protectively around her son. But why would he feel the need to protect Clara Easton? From what he'd learned about her, she was more than capable of taking care of herself. Not to mention that he barely knew her. And he wouldn't be getting to know her any better than he had to after this first encounter.

Sure, it was inevitable that their paths would cross in the future, since his mother would want to see as much of Henry as possible, and Clara would be included in that. But Grant didn't have the time or inclination to be *Uncle Grant*, even without the *Uncle* part. He and Brent might have been identical in looks, but they'd been totally different in every other way. Brent was always the charming, cheerful twin, while Grant was the sober, silent one. Brent made friends with abandon. Grant's few friends barely knew him. Brent treated life like a party. Grant knew it was a chore. Brent loved everyone he ever met. Grant never—

Clara Easton walked past him, leaving in her wake a faint aroma of something spicy and sweet. Cinnamon, he realized. And ginger. She smelled like Christmas morning. Except not the Christmas mornings he knew now, which were only notable because they were a day off from work. She smelled like the Christmas mornings of his childhood, before his father died, when the Dunbartons were happy.

Wow. He hadn't thought about those Christmas mornings for a long time. Because thinking about mornings like that reminded him of a time and place—reminded him of a person—he would never know again. A time when Grant had been staggeringly contented, and when his future had been filled with the promise of—

Of lots of things that never happened. He didn't usually like being reminded of mornings like that. For some reason, though, he didn't mind having Clara Easton and her cinnamon bun–gingerbread scent remind him today. He just wished he was the kind of person who could reciprocate. The kind of person who could be charming and cheerful and made friends with abandon. The kind who treated life like a party and loved everyone he met.

The kind who could draw the eye of a woman like Clara Easton in a way that didn't make her respond with fear and anxiety.

As Clara followed Grant Dunbarton deeper into the penthouse, she told herself she was silly to feel so intimidated. It was just an apartment. Just a really big, really sumptuous apartment. On one of the most expensive streets in the world. Filled with art and antiques with a value that probably exceeded the gross national product of some sovereign nations. She knew nothing of dates or styles when it came to antiques, but she was going to go out on a limb and say the decor here was Early Conspicuous Consumption.

Inescapably, she compared it to her two-bedroom, one-bath apartment above the bakery. Her furniture was old, too, but her Midcentury Salvage wasn't nearly as chic, and her original artwork had been executed by a preschooler. Add to that the general chaos that came with having said preschooler underfoot—and also rocks, puzzle pieces and Cheerios underfoot—and it was pretty clear who had the better living space. She just hoped Hank didn't notice that, too. But judging by the way he walked with his eyes wide, his neck craned and his mouth open, she was pretty sure he did.

"So…how long have y'all lived here?" she asked Grant. Mostly because no one had said a word since she and Hank and Gus entered, and she was beginning to think none of them would ever speak again.

Grant slowed until she pulled alongside him, which was something of a mixed blessing. On the upside, she could see his face. On the downside, she could see his face. And all she could do was be struck again by how much he resembled Brent. Well, that and also worry about how the resemblance set off little explosions in her midsection that warmed places inside her that really shouldn't be warming in mixed company.

"Brent and I grew up here," he said. "The place has been in the family for three generations."

"Wow," Clara said. Talk about having deep roots somewhere. "I grew up in Macon. But I've been living on Tybee Island since I graduated from college."

"Yes, I know," he told her. "You graduated from Carson High School with a near-perfect GPA and have a business administration degree from the College of Coastal Georgia that you earned in three years. Not bad. Especially considering how you worked three jobs the entire time."

Clara told herself she shouldn't be surprised. Families like the Dunbartons didn't open their door to just anyone. "You had me checked out, I see."

"Yes," he admitted without apology. "I'm sure you understand."

Actually, she did. When it came to family—even if that family only numbered two, like her and Hank—

you did what you had to do to protect it. Had August Fiver not already had a ton of info to give her about the Dunbartons, Clara would have had them checked out, too, before allowing them access to her son.

"Well, the AP classes in high school helped a lot with that three-years thing," she told him.

"So did perseverance and hard work."

Well, okay, there was that, too.

Grant led them to a small study that was executed in pale yellow and paler turquoise and furnished with overstuffed moiré chairs, a frilly desk and paintings of gorgeous landscapes. The room reeked of Marie Antoinette—the Versailles version, not the Bastille version—so Clara was pretty sure this wasn't a sanctuary for him.

As if cued by the thought, a woman entered from a door on the other side of the room. This had to be Grant's mother, Francesca. She looked to be in her midfifties, with short, dark hair liberally streaked with silver and eyes as rich a blue as her sons'. She was nearly as tall as Clara, but slimmer, dressed in flowing palazzo pants and tunic the color of a twilit sky. Diamond studs winked in each earlobe, and both wrists were wrapped in silver bracelets. She halted when she saw her guests, her gaze and smile alighting for only a second on Clara before falling to Hank…whereupon her eyes filled with tears.

But her smile brightened as she hurried forward, arms outstretched in the universal body language for *Gimme a big ol' hug*. She halted midstride, however, when Hank stepped backward, pressing himself into Clara with enough force to make her stumble backward herself. Until Grant halted her, wrapping sure fingers around her upper arms. For the scantest of moments, her brain tricked her into thinking it was Brent catching her, and she came *this close* to spinning around to plant a grateful kiss on Grant's mouth, so instinctive was her response.

Was it going to be like this the whole time she was here? Was the younger version of herself that still obviously lived inside her going to keep thinking it was Brent, not Grant, she was interacting with? If so, it was going to be a long week.

"Thanks," she murmured over her shoulder, hoping he didn't hear her breathlessness.

When he didn't release her immediately, she turned around to look at him, an action that caused him to release one shoulder, but not the other. For a moment, they only gazed at each other, and Clara was again overcome by how much he resembled Brent, and how that resemblance roused all kinds of feelings in her she really didn't need to be feeling. Then, suddenly, Grant smiled. But damned if his smile wasn't just like Brent's, too.

"Where are my manners?" he asked, his hand still curved over her arm. "I should have taken your coat the minute you walked in."

Automatically, Clara began to unbutton her coat… then suddenly halted. Because it didn't feel as if she was unbuttoning her coat for a man who had politely asked for it. It felt as if she was unbuttoning her shirt—or dress or skirt or pants or whatever else she might have on—so she could make love with Brent.

Wow. It really was going to be a long week. Maybe she and Hank should just head home tomorrow. Or even before dinner. Or lunch.

She went back to her buttons before her hesitation seemed weird—though, judging by Grant's expression, he already thought it was weird. Beneath her coat, she wore a short black dress and red-and-black polka dot tights that had felt whimsical and Christmassy when she put them on but felt out of place now amid the elegance of the Dunbarton home.

She and Hank should *definitely* leave before lunch.

Her plan was dashed, however, when Francesca, who had stopped a slight distance from Hank but still looked like the happiest woman in the world, said, "It is so lovely to have you both here. I am so glad we found you. Thank you so much for staying with us. I've asked Timmerman to bring up your bags." Obviously not wanting to overwhelm her grandson, she focused on Clara when she spoke again. "You must be Clara," she said as she extended her right hand.

Clara accepted it automatically. "I'm so sorry about Brent, Mrs. Dunbarton. He was a wonderful person."

Francesca's smile dimmed some, but didn't go away. "Yes, he was. And please, call me Francesca." She clasped her hands together when she looked at Hank, as if still not trusting herself to not reach for him. "And you, of course, must be Henry. Hello there, young man."

Hank said nothing for a moment, only continued to lean against Clara as he gave his grandmother wary consideration. Finally, politely, he said, "Hello. My name is Henry. But everybody calls me Hank."

Francesca positively beamed. "Well, then I will, too. And what should we have you call me, Hank?"

This time Hank looked up at Clara, and she could see he had no idea how to respond. They had talked before coming to New York about his father's death and his newly discovered grandmother and uncle, but conveying all the ins and outs of those things to a three-year-old hadn't been easy, and she still wasn't sure how much Hank understood. But when he'd asked if this meant he and Clara would be spending holidays like Thanksgiving and Christmas with his new family, and whether they could come to Tybee Island for his birthday parties, it had finally struck Clara just how big a life change this was going to be for her son.

And for her, too. It had been just the two of them for more than three years. She'd figured it would stay just the two of them for a couple of decades, at least, until Hank found a partner and started a family—and a life—of his own. Clara hadn't expected to have to share him so soon. Or to have to share him with strangers.

Who wouldn't be strangers for long, since they were family—Hank's family, anyway. But that was something else Clara had been forced to accept. Now her son had a family other than her. But she still just had—and would always just have—him.

She tried not to stumble over the words when she said, "Hank, sweetie, this is your grandmother. You two need to figure out what y'all want to call her."

Francesca looked at Hank again, her hands still clasped before her, still giving him the space he needed. Clara was grateful the older woman realized that a child his age needed longer to get used to a situation like this than an adult did. Clara understood well the enormity and exuberance of a mother's love. It was the only kind of love she did understand. It was the only kind she'd ever known. She knew how difficult it was to rein it in. She appreciated Francesca's doing so for her grandson.

"Do you know what your father and Uncle Grant called their grandmother?" Francesca asked Hank.

He shook his head. "No, ma'am. What?"

Francesca smiled at the *No, ma'am*. Clara supposed it wasn't something a lot of children said anymore. But she had been brought up to say *no, ma'am* and *no, sir* when speaking to adults—it was still the Southern way in a lot of places—so it was only natural to teach Hank to say it, too. One small step for courtesy. One giant step for the human race.

"They called her Grammy," Francesca told Hank. "What do you think about calling me Grammy?"

Clara felt Hank relax. "I guess I could call you Grammy, if you think it's okay."

Francesca's eyes went damp again, and she smiled. "I think it would be awesome."

Now Clara smiled, too. The woman had clearly done her homework and remembered how to talk to a child. A grandmother's love must be as enormous and exuberant as a mother's love. Hank could do a lot worse than Francesca Dunbarton for a grandmother.

"Now, then," Francesca said. "Would you like to see your father's old room? It looks just like it did when he wasn't much older than you."

Hank looked at Clara for approval.

"Go ahead, sweetie," she told him. "I'd like to see your dad's room, too." To Francesca, she added, "If you don't mind me tagging along."

"Of course not. Maybe your uncle Grant will come with us. You can, too, Mr. Fiver, if you want to."

Clara turned to the two men, expecting them to excuse themselves due to other obligations, and was surprised to find Grant looking not at his mother, but at her, intently enough that she got the impression he'd been looking at her for some time. A ball of heat somersaulted through her midsection a few times and came to rest in a place just below her heart. Because the way he was looking at her was the same way Brent had looked at her, whenever he was thinking about...well... Whenever he was feeling frisky. And, wow, suddenly, out of nowhere, Clara started feeling a little frisky, too.

He isn't Brent, she reminded herself firmly. He might

look like Brent and sound like Brent and move like Brent, but Grant Dunbarton wasn't the sexy charmer who had taught her to laugh and play and frolic one summer, then given her the greatest gift she would ever receive, in the form of his son. As nice as Grant was trying to be, he would never, could never, be his brother. Of that, Clara was certain. That didn't make him bad. It just made him someone else. Someone who should not—would not, could not, she told herself sternly—make her feel frisky. Even a little.

"Thank you, Mrs. Dunbarton," Gus said, pulling her thoughts back to the matter at hand—and not a moment too soon. "But I should get back to the office. Unless Clara needs me for anything else."

She shook her head. He'd only come this morning to be a buffer between her and the Dunbartons, should one be necessary. But Francesca was being so warm and welcoming, and Grant was *trying* to be warm and welcoming, so… No, Grant *was* warm and welcoming, she told herself. He just wasn't quite as good at it as his mother was. As his brother had been, once upon a time.

"Go ahead, Gus, it's fine," she said. "Thank you for everything you've done. We appreciate it."

He said his goodbyes and told the Dunbartons he could find his own way out. Clara waited for Grant to leave, too, but he only continued to gaze at her in that heated way, looking as if he didn't intend to go anywhere. Not unless she was going with him.

He's not Brent, she told herself again. *He's not.*

Now if only she could convince herself he wouldn't be the temptation his brother had been, too.

Two

Unfortunately, as Francesca led them back the way they'd all come, Grant matched his stride to Clara's and stayed close enough that she could fairly feel the heat of his body mingling with hers and inhale the faint scent of him—something spicy and masculine and nothing like Brent's, which had been a mix of sun and surf and salt. It was just too bad that Grant's fragrance was a lot more appealing. Thankfully, their walk didn't last long. Francesca turned almost immediately down a hallway that ended in a spiral staircase, something that enchanted Hank, because he'd never seen anything like it.

"Are we going up or down?" he asked Francesca.

"Down," she said. "But it can be kind of tricky, and sometimes I get a little wonky. Do you mind if I hold your hand, so I don't fall?"

Hank took his grandmother's hand and promised to keep her safe.

"Oh, thank you, Hank," she gushed. "I can already tell you're going to be a big help around here."

Something in the comment and Francesca's tone gave Clara pause. Both sounded just a tad…proprietary. As if Francesca planned for Hank to be *around here* for a long time. She told herself Francesca was just trying to make things more comfortable between herself and her grandson. And, anyway, what grandmother wouldn't want her grandson to be around? Clara had made clear through Gus that she and Hank would only be in New York for a week. Everything was fine.

Francesca halted by the first closed door Clara had seen in the penthouse. When the other woman curled her fingers over the doorknob, Clara felt like Dorothy Gale, about to go from her black-and-white farmhouse to a Technicolor Oz. And what lay on the other side was nearly as fantastic: a bedroom that was easily five times the size of Hank's at home and crammed with boyish things. Brent must have been clinging to his childhood with both fists when he left home.

One entire wall was nothing but shelves, half of them blanketed by books, the other half teeming with toys. From the ceiling in one corner hung a papier-mâché solar system, low enough that a child could reach up and, with a flick of his wrist, send its planets into orbit. On the far side of the room was a triple bunk bed with both a ladder and a sliding board for access. The walls were covered with maps of far-off places and photos of exotic beasts. The room was full of everything a little boy's heart could ever desire—building blocks, musical instruments, game systems, stuffed animals… They might as well have been in a toy store, so limitless were the choices.

Hank seemed to think so, too. Although he entered

behind Francesca, the minute he got a glimpse of his surroundings, he bulleted past his grandmother in a blur. He spun around in a circle in the middle of the room, taking it all in, then fairly dove headfirst into a bin full of Legos. It could be days before he came up for air.

Clara thought of his bedroom back home. She'd bought his bed at a yard sale and repainted it herself. His toy box was a plastic storage bin—not even the biggest size available—and she'd built his shelves out of wood salvaged from a demolished pier. At home, he had enough train track to make a figure eight. Here, he could re-create the Trans-Siberian Railway. At home, he had enough stuffed animals for Old McDonald's farm. Here, he could repopulate the Earth after the Great Flood.

This was not going to end well when Clara told him it was time for the two of them to go home.

Francesca knelt beside the Lego bin with Hank, plucking out bricks and snapping them together with a joy that gave his own a run for its money. She must have done the same thing with Brent when he was Hank's age. Clara's heart hurt seeing them. She couldn't imagine what it would be like to lose a child. This meeting with her grandson had to be both comforting and heartbreaking for Francesca.

Clara sensed more than saw Grant move to stand beside her. He, too, was watching the scene play out, but Clara could no more guess his thoughts than she could stop the sun from rising. She couldn't imagine losing a sibling, either. Although she'd had "brothers" and "sisters" in a couple of her foster homes, sometimes sharing a situation with them for years, all of them had maintained a distance. No one ever knew when they would be jerked up and moved someplace new, so it was always best not to get too attached to anyone. And none of the kids ever shared the same memories or histories as the others. Everyone came with his or her own—and left with them, too. Sometimes that was all a kid left with. There was certainly never anything like this.

"I can't believe y'all still have this much of Brent's stuff," she said.

Grant shrugged. "My mother was always sure Brent would eventually get tired of his wandering and come home, and she didn't want to get rid of anything he might want to keep. And Brent never threw away anything. Well, no material possessions, anyway," he hastened to clarify.

When his gaze met hers, Clara knew he was backtracking in an effort to not hurt her feelings by suggesting that Brent had thrown away whatever he shared with her.

"It's okay," she said. "Brent and I were never… I mean, there was nothing between us that was…" She stopped, gathered her thoughts and tried again, lowering her voice this time so that Francesca and Hank couldn't hear. "Neither of us wanted or expected anything permanent. There was an immediate attraction, and we could talk for hours, right off the bat, about anything and everything—as long as it didn't go any deeper than the surface. It was one of those things that happens sometimes, where two people just feel comfortable around each other as soon as they meet. Like they were old friends in a previous life or something, picking up where they left off, you know?"

He studied her in silence for a moment, and then shook his head. "No. Nothing like that has ever happened to me."

Clara sobered. "Oh. Well. It was like that for me and Brent. He really was a wonderful person when I knew him. We had a lot of fun together for a few weeks. But neither of us wanted anything more than that. It could have just as easily been me who walked away. He just finished first."

She tried not to chuckle at her wording. Brent finishing first was pretty much par for the course. Not just with their time together, but with their meals together. With their walks together. With their sex together. Yes, that part had been great, too. But he was never able to quite...satisfy her.

"He was always in a hurry," Grant said.

Clara smiled. "Yes, he was."

"He was like a hummingbird when we were kids. The minute his feet hit the ground in the morning, he was unstoppable. There were so many things he wanted to do. Every day, there were so many things. And he never knew where to start, so he just...went. Everywhere. Constantly."

Brent hadn't been as hyper as that when she met him, but he'd never quite seemed satisfied with anything, either, as if there was something else, something better, somewhere else. He told her he left home at eighteen and had been tracing the coastline of North America ever since, starting in Nome, Alaska, heading south, and then skipping from San Diego to Corpus Christi for the Gulf of Mexico. When she asked him where he would go next, he said he figured he'd keep going as far north into Newfoundland as he could, and then hop over to Scandinavia and start following Europe's shoreline. Then he'd do Asia's. Then Africa's. Then South America's. Then, who knew?

"He was still restless when I met him," she told Grant. "But I always thought his restlessness was like mine."

He eyed her curiously, and her heart very nearly stopped beating. His expression was again identical to Brent's, whenever he puzzled over something. She wondered if she would ever be able to look at Grant and *not* see Hank's father. Then again, it wasn't as if she'd be looking at him forever. Yes, she was sure to see Grant again after she and Hank left New York, since Francesca would want regular visits, but Clara's interaction with him would be minimal. Still, she hoped at some point her heart would stop skipping a beat whenever she looked at him. Odd, since she couldn't remember it skipping this much when she looked at Brent.

"What do you mean?" he asked.

"I thought his restlessness was because he came from the same kind of situation I did, where he never stayed in one place for very long so couldn't get rooted for any length of time. Like maybe he was an army brat or his parents were itinerant farmers or something."

Now Grant's expression turned to one of surprise. And damned if it didn't look just like Brent's would have, too. "He never told you anything about his past? About his family?"

"Neither of us talked about anything like that. There was some unspoken rule where we both recognized that it was off-limits to talk about anything too personal. I knew why I didn't want to talk about my past. I figured his reasons must have been the same."

"Because of the foster homes and children's institutions," Grant said. "That couldn't have been a happy experience for you."

She told herself she shouldn't be surprised he knew about that, too. Of course his background check would have been thorough. In spite of that, she said, "You really did do your homework."

He said nothing, only treated her to an unapologetic shrug.

"What else did you find out?" she asked.

He started to say something, then hesitated. But somehow, the look on his face told Clara he knew a lot more than she wanted him to know. And since he had the finances and, doubtless, contacts to uncover everything he could, he'd probably uncovered the one thing she'd never told anyone about herself.

Still keeping her voice low, so that Francesca and Hank couldn't hear, she asked, "You know where I was born, don't you? And the circumstances of why I was born in that particular location."

He nodded. "Yeah. I do."

Which meant he knew she was born in the Bibb County jail to a nineteen-year-old girl who was awaiting trial for her involvement in an armed robbery she had committed with Clara's father. He might even know—

"Do you know the part about who chose my name?" she asked further, still in the low tone that ensured only Grant would hear her.

He nodded. "One of the guards named you after the warden's mother because your own mother didn't name you at all." Wow. She'd had no idea he would dig that deep. All he'd had to do was make sure she was gainfully employed, reasonably well educated and didn't have a criminal record herself. He hadn't needed to bring her— She stopped herself before thinking the word *family*, since the people who had donated her genetic material might be related to her, but they would never be family. Anyway, he hadn't needed to learn about them, too. They'd had nothing to do with her life after generating it.

"And I know that after she and your father were convicted," he continued in a low tone of his own, "there was no one else in the family able to care for you."

Thankfully, he left out the part about how that was because the rest of her relatives were either addicted, incarcerated or missing. Though she didn't doubt he knew all that, too. She listened for traces of contempt or revulsion in his voice but heard neither. He was as matter-of-fact about the unpleasant circumstances of her birth and parentage as he would have been were he reading a how-to manual for replacing a carburetor. As matter-of-fact about those things as she was herself, really. She should probably give him kudos for that. It bothered Clara, though—a lot—that he knew so many details about her origins.

Which was something else to add to the That's Weird list, because she had never really cared about anyone knowing those details before. She would have even told Brent, if he'd asked. She knew it wasn't her fault that her parents weren't the cream of society. And she didn't ask to be born, especially into a situation like that. She'd done her best to not let any of it hold her back, and she thought she'd done a pretty good job.

Evidently, Grant didn't hold her background against her, either, because when he spoke again, it was in that same even tone. "You spent your childhood mostly in foster care, but in some group homes and state homes, too. When they cut you loose at eighteen, where a lot of kids would have hit the streets and gotten into trouble, you got those three jobs and that college degree. Last year, you bought the bakery where you were working when its owner retired, and you've already made it more profitable. Just barely, but profit is an admirable accomplishment. Especially in this economic climate. So bravo, Clara Easton."

His praise made her feel as if she was suddenly the cream of society. More weirdness. "Thanks," she said.

He met her gaze longer than was necessary for acknowledgment, and the jumble of feelings inside her got jumbled up even more. "You're welcome," he said softly.

Their gazes remained locked for another telling moment—at least, it was telling for Clara, but what it mostly told her was that it had been way too long since she'd been out on a date—then she made herself look back at the scene in the bedroom. By now, Francesca was seated on the floor alongside Hank, holding the base of a freeform creation that he was building out in a new direction—sideways.

"He'll never be an engineer at this rate," Clara said. "That structure is in no way sound."

"What do you think he will be?" Grant asked.

"I have no clue," she replied. "He'll be whatever he decides he wants to be."

When she looked at Grant again, he was still studying her with great interest. But there was something in his eyes that hadn't been there before. Clara had no idea how she knew it, but in that moment, she did: Grant Dunbarton wasn't a happy guy. Even with all the money, beauty and privilege he had in his life.

She opened her mouth to say something—though, honestly, she wasn't really sure what—when Hank called out, "Mama! I need you to hold this part that Grammy can't!"

Francesca smiled. "Hank's vision is much too magnificent for a mere four hands. My grandson is brilliant, obviously."

Clara smiled back. Hank was still fine-tuning his small motor skills and probably would be for some time. But she appreciated Francesca's bias.

She looked at Grant. "C'mon. You should help, too. If I know Hank, this thing is going to get even bigger."

For the first time since she'd met him, Grant Dunbarton looked rattled. He took a step backward, as if in retreat, even though all she'd done was invite him to join in playtime. She might as well have just asked him to drink hemlock, so clear was his aversion.

"Ah, thanks, but, no," he stammered. He took another step backward, into the hallway. "I… I have a lot of, uh, work. That I need to do. Important work. For work."

"Oh," she said, still surprised by the swiftness with which he lost his composure. Even more surprising was the depth of her disappointment that he was leaving. "Okay. Well. I guess I'll see you later, then. I mean… Hank and I will see you later."

He nodded once—or maybe it was a twitch—then took another step that moved him well and truly out of the bedroom and into the hallway. Clara went the other way, taking her seat on the other side of Hank. When she looked back at the door, though, Grant still hadn't left to do all the important work that he needed to do. Instead, he stood in the hallway gazing at her and Hank and Francesca.

And, somehow, Clara couldn't help thinking he looked less like a high-powered executive who needed to get back to work than he did a little boy who hadn't been invited to the party.

Grant hadn't felt like a child since… Well, he couldn't remember feeling like a child even when he *was* a child. And he certainly hadn't since his father's death shortly after his tenth birthday. But damned if he didn't feel like one now, watching Clara and her son play on the floor with his mother. It was the way a child felt when he was picked last in gym or ate alone at lunch. Which was nuts, because he'd excelled at sports, and he'd had plenty of friends in school. The fact that they were sports he hadn't really cared about excelling at—but that looked good on a college application—and the fact that he'd never felt all that close to his friends was beside the point.

So why did he suddenly feel so dejected? And so rejected by Clara? Hell, she'd invited him to join them. And how could she be rejecting him when he hadn't even asked her for anything?

Oh, for God's sake. This really was nuts. He should be working. He should have been working the entire time he was standing here revisiting a past it was pointless to revisit. He'd become the CEO of Dunbarton Industries the minute the ink on his MBA dried and hadn't stopped for so much as a coffee break since. Staying home today to meet Clara and Hank with his mother was the first nonholiday weekday he'd spent away from the office in years.

He glanced at his watch. It wasn't even noon. He'd lost less than half a day. He could still go in to the office and get way more done than he would trying to work here. He'd only stayed home in case Clara turned out to be less, ah, stable than her résumé let on and created a problem. But the woman was a perfectly acceptable candidate for mothering a Dunbarton. Well, as an individual, she was. Her family background, on the other hand…

Grant wasn't a snob. At least, he didn't think he was. But when he'd discovered Clara was born in a county jail, and that her parents were currently doing time for other crimes they'd committed… Well, suffice it to say felony convictions weren't exactly pluses on the social register. Nor were they the kind of thing he wanted associated with the Dunbarton name. Not that Hank went by Dunbarton. Well, not yet, anyway. Grant was sure his mother would get around to broaching the topic of changing his last name to theirs eventually. And he was sure Clara would capitulate. What mother wouldn't want her child to bear one of the most respected names in the country?

Having met Clara, however, he was surprised to have another reaction about her family history. He didn't want that sort of thing attached to her name, either. She seemed like too decent a person to have come from that kind of environment. She really had done well for herself, considering her origins. In fact, a lot of people who'd had better breeding and greater fortune than she hadn't gone nearly as far.

He lingered at the bedroom door a minute more, watching the scene before him. No, not watching the scene, he realized. Watching Clara. She was laughing at something his mother had said, while keeping a close eye on Hank who, without warning, suddenly bent and brushed a kiss on his mother's cheek—for absolutely no reason Grant could see. He was stunned by the gesture, but Clara only laughed some more, indicating that this was something her son did often. Then, when in spite of their best efforts, the structure he'd been building toppled to the floor, she wrapped her arms around him, pulled him into her lap and kissed him loudly on the side of his neck. He giggled ferociously, but reached behind himself to hug her close. Then he scrambled out of her clutches and hurried across the room to try his hand at something else.

The entire affectionate exchange lasted maybe ten seconds and was in no way extraordinary. Except that it was extraordinary, because Grant had never shared that kind of affection with his own mother, even before his father's death changed all of them. He'd never shared that kind of affection with anyone. Affection that was so spontaneous, so uninhibited, so lacking in contrivance and conceit. So…so natural. As if it were as vital to them both as breathing.

That, finally, made him walk down the hall to his office. Work. That was what he needed. Something that was as vital to him as breathing. Though maybe he wouldn't go in to the offices of Dunbarton Industries today. Maybe he should stay closer to home. Just in case… Just in case Clara really wasn't all that stable. Just in case she did create a problem. Well, one bigger than the one she'd already created just by being so spontaneous, so uninhibited, so lacking in contrivance and conceit, and so natural. He should still stay home today. Just in case.

You never knew when something extraordinary might happen.

Three

Actually, something extraordinary did happen. On Clara and Hank's second day in New York, the Dunbartons had dinner in the formal dining room. Maybe that didn't sound all that extraordinary—and wouldn't have been a couple of decades ago, because the Dunbartons had always had dinner in the formal dining room before his father's death—but it was now. Because now, the formal dining room was only used for special occasions. Christmas Day, Easter, Thanksgiving, or those few instances when Brent had deigned to make time for a visit home during his hectic schedule of bumming around on the world's best beaches.

Then again, Grant supposed the arrival of a new family member was a special occasion, too. But it was otherwise a regular day, at least for him. He'd spent it at work while his mother had taken Clara and Hank to every New York City icon they could see in a day, from the Staten Island Ferry to the Statue of Liberty to the Empire State Building to whatever else his mother had conjured up.

Grant had always liked the formal dining room a lot better than the smaller one by the kitchen, in spite of its formality. Or maybe because of it. The walls were painted a deep, regal gold, perfectly complementing the long table, chairs and buffet, which were all overblown Louis Quatorze.

But the ceiling was really the centerpiece, with its sweeping painting of the night sky, where the solar system played only one small part in the center, with highlights of the Milky Way fanning out over the rest—constellations and nebulae, with the occasional comet and meteor shower thrown in for good measure. When he was a kid, Grant loved to sneak in here and lie on his back on the rug, looking up at the stars and pretending—

Never mind. It wasn't important what he loved to pretend when he was a kid. He did still love the room, though. And something inside him still made him want to lie on his back on the rug and look up at the stars and pretend—

"It's pretty cool, isn't it?" he asked Hank, who was seated directly across from him, his neck craned back so he could scan the ceiling from one end to the other.

"It's awesome," the little boy said without taking his eyes off it. "Look, Mama, there's Saturn," he added, pointing up with one hand and reaching blindly with the other toward the place beside him to pat his mother's arm…and hitting the flatware instead.

Clara mimicked his posture, tipping her head back to look up. The position left her creamy neck exposed, something Grant tried not to notice. He also tried not to notice how the V-neck of her sweater was low enough to barely hint at the upper swells of her breasts, or how its color—pale blue—brought out a new dimension to her uniquely colored eyes, making them seem even greener somehow. Or how the light from the chandelier set iridescent bits of blue dancing in her black curls. Or how much he wanted to reach over and wind one around his finger to see if it was as soft as it looked.

"Yes, it is," she said in response to Hank's remark. "And what's that big one beside it?"

"Jupiter," he said.

"Very good," Grant told him, unable to hide his surprise and thankful for something else to claim his attention that didn't involve Clara. Or her creamy skin. Or her incredible eyes. Or her soft curls. "You're quite the astronomer, Hank."

"Well, he's working on it," Clara said with a smile. "Those are the only two planets he knows so far."

Grant's mother smiled, too, from her seat at the head of the table. "I have the smartest grandson in the universe. Not that I'm surprised, mind you, considering his paternity." Hastily, she looked at Clara and added, "And his maternity, too, of course!"

Clara smiled and murmured her thanks for the acknowledgment, but his mother continued to beam at her only grandchild. *Only* in more ways than one, Grant thought, since Hank was also likely the only grandchild she would ever have. No way was he suited to the role of father himself. Or husband, for that matter. And neither role appealed. He was, for lack of a better cliché, married to his business. His only offspring would be the bottom line.

"I also know Earth," Hank said, sounding insulted that his mother would overlook that.

Clara laughed. "So you do," she agreed.

Frankly, Grant couldn't believe a three-year-old would know any of the things Hank knew. Then again, when Grant was three, he knew the genus and species of the chambered nautilus—*Nautilus pompilius*. He'd loved learning all about marine life when he was a kid, but the nautilus was a particular favorite from the start, thanks to an early visit to the New York Aquarium where he'd been mesmerized by the animal. If a child discovered his passion early in life, there was no way to prevent him from absorbing facts like a sponge, even at three. Evidently, for Hank, astronomy would be such a passion.

"Do you have a telescope?" Grant asked Clara.

She shook her head. "If he stays interested in astronomy, we can invest in one. He can save his allowance and contribute. For now, binoculars are fine."

Hank nodded, seeming in no way bothered by the delay. So not expecting instant gratification was something else he'd inherited from his mother. Brent's life had been nothing *but* a demand for instant gratification.

Yet Clara could afford to give him instant gratification now. She could afford to buy her son a telescope with his newfound wealth, whether he stayed interested in astronomy or not. But she wasn't. Grant supposed she was trying to ensure that Hank didn't fall into the trap his father had. She didn't want him to think that just because he had money, he no longer had to work to earn something, that he could take advantage and have whatever he wanted, wherever and whenever he wanted it. Grant's estimation of her rose. Again.

As if he'd said the words out loud, she looked at him and smiled. Or maybe she did that because she was grateful he hadn't told her son that if he wanted a telescope, then, by God, he should have one, cost be damned. That was what Brent would have done. Then he would have scooped up Hank after dinner and taken him straight to Telescopes "R" Us to buy him the biggest, shiniest, most expensive one they had, without even bothering to see if it was the best.

As Hank and Francesca fell into conversation about the other planets on the ceiling, Grant turned to Clara. And realized he had no idea what to say to her. So he fell back on the obvious.

"Brent had an interest in astronomy when he was Hank's age, too," he told her. "It was one of the reasons my mother had this room decorated the way she did."

"I actually knew that," Clara said. "About the astronomy, not the room. He took me to Skidaway Island a few times to look at the stars. I've taken Hank, too. It's what started his interest in all this."

Grant nodded. Of course Brent would have taken her to a romantic rendezvous to dazzle her with his knowledge of the stars. And of course she would carry that memory with her and share it with their son.

"Hank is now about the same age I was when I started getting interested in baking," she said. "My foster mother at that time baked a lot, and she let me help her in the kitchen. I remember being amazed at how you could mix stuff together to make a gooey mess only to have it come out of the oven as cake. Or cookies. Or banana bread. Or whatever. And I loved how pretty everything was after the frosting went on. And how you could use the frosting to make it even prettier, with roses or latticework or ribbons. It was like making art. Only you could eat it afterward."

As she spoke about learning to bake, her demeanor changed again. Her eyes went dreamy, her cheeks grew rosy, and she seemed to go…softer somehow. All over. And she gestured as she spoke—something she didn't even seem aware of doing—stirring an imaginary bowl when she talked about the gooey mess, and opening an imaginary oven door when she talked about the final product and tracing a flower pattern on the tablecloth as she spoke of using frosting as an art medium. He was so caught up in the play of her hands and her storytelling, that he was completely unprepared when she turned the tables on him.

"What were you interested in when you were that age?"

The question hung in the air between them for a moment as Grant tried to form a response. Then he realized he didn't know how to respond. For one thing, he didn't think it was a question anyone had ever asked him before. For another, it had been so long since he'd thought about his childhood, he honestly couldn't remember.

Except he *had* remembered. A few minutes ago, when he'd been thinking about how fascinated he'd been by the chambered nautilus. About how much he'd loved all things related to marine life when he was a kid. Which was something he hadn't thought about in years.

Despite that, he said, "I don't know. The usual stuff, I guess."

His childhood love was so long ago, and he'd never pursued it beyond the superficial. Even though, he supposed, knowing the biological classification of the entire nautilus family—in Latin—by the time he started first grade went a little beyond superficial. That was different. Because that was…

Well, it was just different, that was all.

"Nothing in particular," he finally concluded. Even if that didn't feel like a conclusion at all.

Clara didn't seem to think so, either, because she insisted, "Oh, come on. There must have been something. All of Hank's friends have some kind of passion. With Brianna, it's seashells. With Tyler, it's rocks. With Megan, it's fairies. It's amazing the single-minded devotion a kid that age can have for something."

For some reason, Grant wanted very much to change the subject. So he turned the tables back on Clara. "So, owning a bakery. That must be gratifying, taking your childhood passion and making a living out of it as an adult."

For a moment, he didn't think Clara was going to let him get away with changing the subject. She eyed him narrowly, with clear speculation, nibbling her lower lip—that ripe, generous, delectable lower lip—in thought.

Just when Grant thought he might climb over the table to nibble it, too, she stopped and said, "It is gratifying."

He'd just bet it was. Oh, wait. She meant the bakery thing, not the lip-nibbling thing.

"Except that when your passion becomes your job," she went on, "it can sort of rob it of the fun, you know? I mean, it's still fun, but some of the magic is gone."

Magic, he repeated to himself. *Fun*. When was the last time he had a conversation with a woman—or, hell, anyone—that included either of those words? Yet here was Clara Easton, using them both in one breath.

"Don't get me wrong," she hastened to clarify. "I do love it. I just…"

She sighed with something akin to wistfulness. Damn. *Wistfulness*. There was another word Grant could never recall coming up in a conversation before—even in his head.

"Sometimes," she continued, "I just look at all the stuff in the bakery kitchen and at all the pastries out in the shop, and, after work, I go upstairs to the apartment with Hank, and I wonder… Is that it? Have I already peaked? I have this great kid, and we have a roof over our heads and food in the pantry, and I'm doing for a living what I always said I wanted to do, and yet sometimes… Sometimes—"

"—It's not enough," Grant said at the same time she did.

Her eyes widened in surprise at his completion of her thoughts, but she nodded. "Yeah. So you do understand."

He started to deny it. Was she crazy? Of course he had enough. He was a Dunbarton. He'd been born with more than enough. Loving parents. A brother who, had life worked the way it was supposed to, would have been a lifelong friend. Piles of money. All the best toys. All the best schools. Not to mention every possible opportunity life could offer waiting for him around every corner. And yet… And yet.

"Yeah, I do understand," he told her.

"So you must be doing something you love, too," she said.

Damn. She had turned the tables again. But his response was automatic. "Of course I love it. It's what I was brought up to do. It's the family business. Dunbartons have loved it for generations. Why wouldn't I love it?"

Belatedly, he realized how defensive he sounded. Clara obviously thought so, too, because her dreamy expression became considerably less dreamy. He searched for words that would make the dreaminess return—

since he'd really liked that look, probably more than he should—but he couldn't think of a single one. They'd already used up *magic*, *fun* and *wistfulness*. Grant wasn't sure he knew any other words like that.

Then he considered Clara again and was flooded with them. Words like *delightful*. And *luscious*. And *enchanting*. They were words he never used. But somehow, they and more like them all rushed to the fore, until his brain felt as if it was turning into a thesaurus. A purple thesaurus, at that.

Fortunately, their cook, Mrs. Bentley, arrived with the first course, and Clara was complimenting the dish and thanking Mrs. Bentley for her trouble. Grant started to point out that it wasn't any trouble, since that was Mrs. Bentley's job and had been for years, and she was being paid well for it. Then he remembered that Clara prepared food for a living, so expressing gratitude for it was probably some kind of professional courtesy. It also occurred to him that he was suddenly in a really irritable mood. But the subject of childhood passions evaporated after that, something for which he was grateful.

Now if only he could get rid of his troubling thoughts as easily.

Clara didn't think she'd ever been happier to see a salad than she was when the Dunbartons' cook placed one in front of her. Of course, the woman could have placed a live scorpion in front of her, and Clara would have been happy to see it. Anything to break her gaze away from Grant's. Because never had she seen anyone look more desolate than he did when he was talking about what he did for a living.

And he couldn't remember what he loved most as a child. Who didn't remember that? Everyone had loved something more than anything else when they were a kid. Everyone had wanted to be something more than anything else when they grew up. For Clara, it had been a baker. For Hank, at the moment, it was an astronomer. For Brent, it had been an astronaut. Even if it was something as unlikely as zookeeper or movie star, every child had some dream of becoming something. Of becoming someone. Every child, evidently, except Grant Dunbarton.

Then again, when a family had owned a business for generations, like the Dunbartons had, maybe it was just a given that their children's professional destiny lay in that business. Except that Brent hadn't gone to work for Dunbarton Industries. He'd been a professional vagabond, which was about as far removed from corporate kismet as a person could get. And he and Grant were the same age, so it wasn't as if taking over the business was a firstborn offspring responsibility for which Grant specifically had been groomed since birth. Nor did Francesca strike Clara as the kind of parent who would insist that her children pursue a preplanned agenda for the sake of the family. If Grant had shouldered the mantle of CEO for Dunbarton Industries, he must have done so because he wanted to.

Even if he didn't look or sound as if he'd wanted to.

The moment was now gone, however. Which was good for another reason, since it kept Clara from wondering if that was what the Dunbartons might have in mind for Hank. He was as much a Dunbarton as Grant and Francesca were. So he was as much a part of the family heritage—and family business—as they were. Surely they didn't have expectations like that for him, though. Although their blood ran in his veins, their society didn't. Nor would it ever, since there was no way

Clara would uproot her son from Georgia and move him to New York.

Even in Georgia, she planned to shield him from this world as much as she could. She didn't have anything against rich people—at least not the ones who earned their wealth and paid their employees a decent wage and gave something back to the community that had helped them build their empire. But the world those people lived in wasn't the real world or real life any more than Clara's upbringing had been.

And she wanted Hank to have a real life. One that involved both hard work and fun play, both discipline and reward. One where he would experience at least some anguish and heartache, because that was the only way to experience serenity and joy. It was impossible to appreciate the latter without knowing the former. And a person couldn't know the former if he was handed everything he wanted on a silver platter.

Maybe that was Grant's problem, she thought, sneaking another look at him. He was blandly forking around his salad, looking way more somber than a person should look when blandly forking around a salad. Maybe by having everything he'd ever wanted all his life, he was incapable of really *knowing* what he wanted. Except that he hadn't had everything he wanted, she thought. He'd lost his father when he was a child, and had lost his twin brother less than a year ago. He'd just told her how he understood what it was to not have enough, and she had a feeling there was more to it than just his personal losses.

She told herself to stop trying to figure him out. Grant Dunbarton's unhappiness and lack of fulfillment were none of her business, and they weren't her responsibility. She reminded herself again—why did she have to keep doing that?—that her life and his were only intersecting temporarily for now and would only be intersecting sporadically in the future. He wasn't her concern.

So why couldn't she stop feeling so concerned about him?

Four

Beware the Park Avenue doyenne with a platinum credit card. That was the only thought circling through Clara's head at the end of her third day in New York, probably because she was so exhausted at that point that it was the only thought that *could* circle through her brain. Francesca Dunbarton was a dynamo when it came to spending money.

As Clara lay beside a sleeping Hank in Brent's old bedroom, she did her best to not nod off herself. No easy feat, that, since the three of them had hit every place Francesca insisted they needed to hit so her only grandchild would have all the essentials of other Park Avenue grandchildren: Boomerang Toys and Books of Wonder, Bit'z Kids and Sweet William, the Disney Store, the Lego Store…pretty much anything a three-year-old would love with the word *store* attached to it.

Then Francesca had insisted they *must* do the

Children's Tea at the Russian Tea Room, because Hank would find it enchanting. They just had *so* much catching up to do!

Hank had finally succumbed to fatigue on the cab ride home and hadn't stirred since. Not when the elevator dinged their arrival on the top floor, not when Clara laid him on the bed, not when Francesca brushed a kiss on his cheek, not when the doorman arrived to deliver all the bags containing his grandmother's purchases for him. And those bags had rattled *a lot.* And there were *a lot* of bags to rattle.

Now Clara lay beside Hank, her elbow braced on the mattress, her head cradled in her hand, and as she watched the hypnotic rise and fall of her son's chest, her eyelids began to flutter. Until she heard the jangle of something metallic and the fall of footsteps in the hallway beyond the open door. Grant, arriving home from work. He appeared in the doorway wearing an impeccable dark suit, tie and dress shirt, the uniform of the upper-crust environment in which he thrived. It was Clara, in her olive drab cargo pants and oatmeal-colored sweater, not to mention her stocking feet, who was out of place here.

When he saw her, Grant lifted a hand in greeting and was about to say something out loud, but halted when he saw Hank sleeping so soundly. Clara lifted her finger in a silent *Hang on a sec*, then carefully maneuvered herself around Hank until she could slide to the floor and tiptoe toward the door and into the hall.

"You didn't have to get up," he said softly by way of a greeting.

"That's okay," she told him. "I needed to get up. I was about to doze off myself."

"Go ahead. Dinner won't be ready for another few hours, at least."

She shook her head. "If I sleep now, I won't sleep tonight. And I'm already a terrible insomniac as it is. I have been since I was a kid."

Because growing up, there had just been something about sharing a room with other kids she didn't know well that lent itself to lousy sleep habits. Clara's experiences in foster care and group homes hadn't been horrible, but most of them hadn't been especially great, either. She'd been the victim of theft and bullying and rivalry like many children—even those who weren't wards of the state—all things that could create stress and wariness in a kid and contribute to insomnia. Sure, none of those things was a part of her life now, but it was hard to undo decades' worth of conditioning.

She and Grant studied each other for a moment in strained silence. It was just so difficult to take her eyes off him, just so strange, seeing the mirror image of Brent dressed in the antithesis of Brent's wardrobe. And the close-cropped hair, in addition to being nothing like Brent's nearly shoulder-length tresses, was peppered with premature silver. She wondered if Brent had started to go gray, too, in the years since she had seen him, or if Grant's gray was simply the result of a more stressful life than his brother had led.

Then the gist of his words struck her, and she smiled. "A few hours till dinner? You must be home earlier than usual, then."

She meant for the comment to be teasing. Evidently, Grant wasn't the workaholic she'd assumed if he ended his office hours early enough to have some relaxation time before dinner. The realization heartened her. Maybe he did have something in common with his twin.

But Grant seemed to take the comment at face value. "Yeah, I am, actually," he said matter-of-factly. "But I could bring the work home with me, and I thought maybe you—and Hank, too, for that matter—I thought both of you, actually, might…um…"

Somehow, she knew he'd intended to end the sentence with the words *need me*, but decided at the last minute to say something else instead. No other words came out of his mouth, though.

Clara had trouble figuring out what to say next, too, mostly because she was too busy drowning in the deep blue depths of his eyes. Looking into Grant's eyes somehow felt different from looking into Brent's eyes, even though their eyes were identical. There was more intensity, more perception, more comprehension, more, well, depth. She'd never felt as if Brent was looking into her soul, even though the two of them were intimately involved for weeks. But having spent only a short time in Grant's presence, she felt as if he were peering past her surface—or at least trying to—to figure out what lay in her deepest inner self. It was…disconcerting. But not entirely unpleasant.

"Um," she said, struggling to find anything that would break the odd spell. But the only thing that came to mind was something about how beautiful his eyes were, and how very different from his brother's, and how she honestly wasn't sure she ever wanted to stop looking into his eyes, and…well…that probably wasn't something she should say to him right now. Or ever.

Thankfully, he broke eye contact and glanced beyond her into Hank's room—or, rather, Brent's old room, she hastily corrected herself—and said, "Looks like my mother did her share to bump up the gross domestic income today."

Clara turned around to follow his gaze. The pile of bags on the floor seemed to have multiplied in the few minutes since she'd last looked at it. Once again, she was reminded of how much more the Dunbartons could offer her son than she could. Materially, anyway. They'd never be able to love him more than she did. But when one was three years old, it wasn't difficult to let the material render the emotional less valuable. Especially when the material included a toy fire truck with motion-activated lights and sound effects.

"I cannot believe how much stuff she bought for Hank," Clara said. She looked at Grant again. "She really shouldn't have done that. I mean, Hank is extremely grateful—and I am, too," she hastened to add. "But..." She couldn't help the sigh that escaped her, nor could she prevent it from sounding melancholy. "I don't know how we're going to get everything home."

"Leave most of it here," Grant said. "Hank can take home his favorites and play with the rest of it when he comes back to visit." He smiled. "That was probably Mom's intention in the first place."

The thought had crossed Clara's mind, too. More than once. As many times as she'd tried to excuse Francesca's excessive purchasing by telling herself Hank's grandmother was just trying to make up for lost time, Clara hadn't been able to keep herself from wondering if all the gifts were bribes of a sort, to ensure that Hank would badger his mother to bring him back to New York ASAP. Having Grant pretty much confirm her suspicions did nothing to make Clara feel better.

Hank stirred on the bed, murmuring a sleepy complaint, and then turned from one side to the other and settled into slumber again. So Clara pulled the door closed to keep him from being awakened by her conversation with Grant.

"We can talk in my room," he said.

Clara scrambled for an excuse as to why she wouldn't be able to do that, but couldn't come up with a single one. Then she wondered why she was trying, since there had been nothing untoward in his invitation. Brain exhaustion, she told herself. She was too tired to follow him, but too tired to find a reason not to follow him. It had nothing to do with the fact that she just maybe kind of wanted to follow him, for a reason that might possibly be slightly untoward on her part.

So follow him she did, to the room next to Brent's. Even though it was next door, it seemed to take forever to get there; this place was enormous. Grant's room was the same size as Brent's, with the same two arched, floor-to-ceiling windows looking down on the same view of Park Avenue and, beyond it, Central Park.

The similarities ended there, however. Where Brent's room was painted a boyish bright blue, Grant's was the color of café mocha. And where Brent's curtains where patterned in whimsical moons and stars, Grant's were a luxe fabric that shimmered with dozens of earth tones. The furniture was sturdy mahogany—a massive sleigh bed, dressers and nightstands, as well as the bare essentials of manhood: alarm clock, lamps, dish for spare change and keys.

The only bit of color in the room was an aquarium opposite the bed. It was far bigger than anything Clara had ever seen in a pet store, and it was populated by fish in all sizes and colors, darting about as if oblivious to the glass walls that enclosed them.

Clara was drawn to it immediately. Even living so close to the water, she'd never seen so many fish in one place, and the brilliant colors and dynamic motion captivated her. Vaguely, she noted that Grant entered the room behind her, tossed his briefcase onto the bed and approached a wooden valet in the far corner of the room. Vaguely, she noted how he began to loosen his tie and unbutton his shirt, and—

Whoa. Whoa, whoa, whoa, *whoa.* No, she didn't note that vaguely. She noted that *very clearly.* Grant undressing caught Clara's attention in much the same way a tornado swirling toward her front door would catch her attention, and she spun around nearly as quickly. Even if—she was pretty sure—he wouldn't go any further than unfastening his shirt a couple of buttons below the collar or rolling up his sleeves, he was still undressing. And that tended to have an effect on a woman who hadn't seen a man undress for a while. A long while. A *really* long while. Especially a woman who had always enjoyed watching a man undress. A lot. A *whole* lot.

Although his movements were in no way provocative, heat flared in her belly at the sight of him. With an elegant shrug, he slipped off his jacket, then freed the buttons of his shirt cuffs and rolled each up to mid-forearm, exposing muscles that bunched and relaxed with every gesture. As he slung his jacket over the valet, she noted the breadth of his shoulders, too, and, couldn't help remembering the last time she had seen shoulders and arms like his. Except those shoulders and arms had been naked, and they had been hot and damp with perspiration beneath her fingertips. They had belonged to Grant's brother, who had been lying on top of her, gasping.

She remembered, too well, how that had felt—too good—and her face grew warm as her blood rushed faster through her veins. The heat multiplied when

Grant lifted a hand to his necktie and freed it, and then slowly, slowly…oh, so slowly…dragged the length of silk from beneath his collar to drape it over the jacket. But it was when his hands moved to his shirt buttons, loosening first one, then two, then three, that Clara felt as if her entire body would burst into flame. Because she couldn't stop watching those hands, those big, skillful, seductive hands, and remembering how they had felt on—and in—her body.

No, not those hands, she reminded herself. It had been Brent's hands that made her feel that way. Even if, on some level, she suspected Grant was every bit as skilled as his brother when it came to making a woman feel aroused and sexy and shameless and wanton and… and…and…

Um, where was she? Oh, yeah. Fish.

Except she wasn't thinking about fish. Because she was too busy wondering if sex with Grant would be as fierce and incendiary as it had been with Brent, and if it would leave her wanting more—

"…and firemouth."

It took Clara a minute to realize it was Grant who had spoken, and not Brent, so lost had she been in her memories of making love to the latter. Apparently he'd been speaking for some time, too, and might have even called her something that sounded a lot like *firemouth*. But how could he have known what she was thinking?

She gazed at him in silence, hoping her expression revealed nothing of the graphic images that had been tumbling through her brain. But when his gaze finally connected with hers, his smile fell and his eyes went wide, and she was pretty sure he could tell down to the last hot, sweaty detail *exactly* what she had been thinking since she started watching him undress, which meant that whole firemouth thing wasn't too far off the mark. So she did the only thing she could.

She spun quickly away from him, focused on the aquarium, and asked, "What kind of fish are these?" In an effort to look as if she was truly fascinated by the little swimmers, she even bent over and brought her face to within an inch of the glass.

Belatedly, she realized the idiocy of the question. Not only because thanks to her, *both* of them were now doubtless thinking about sex, not fish, but also because asking it caused him to move closer to her. He did so slowly and uncertainly, as if he were approaching a barracuda, which wasn't that far off the mark, really, since, at the moment, she was feeling more than a little predatory.

Breathe, Clara, breathe, she instructed herself. *And calm down.*

Unfortunately, it was impossible for her to do either, because, by then, Grant had moved behind her, his pelvis situated within inches of her, well, behind. If he'd wanted, he could have tugged the drawstring at her waist and pulled down her pants right there. Then he could have tugged down her panties, too, to expose her in the most intimate, most vulnerable way. Then he could have unfastened his belt, unzipped his fly and freed himself. He could have gripped her naked flesh and pulled her toward himself, and then buried himself inside her, slowly, deeply, possessively. Over and over and over again.

If he wanted.

Because in that moment, Clara wouldn't have stopped him, since she suddenly wanted him, too.

Oh, no. Oh, God. Oh, Grant.

Instead, he stepped to her left and bent forward, his

face scant inches from hers, to gaze into the aquarium with her.

She told herself that had been his intention all along. He couldn't possibly have been thinking about doing all the things she had been thinking about him doing. Her brain was just a muddle of memories about her time with Brent—most of which had been spent in sexual pursuits, she had to admit—and was transferring those desires to Grant. She'd known the man a matter of days. Then again, she'd been steaming up the sheets with Brent within hours of meeting him…

"I was just telling you the names of the fish," he said. She could tell he was struggling to keep his voice even and quiet.

"The one in front," he continued, "well, the one that was in front a minute ago, when you were, ah, looking at him, is a firemouth."

Ah. So he hadn't been calling Clara that. At least she didn't think he had. Probably best to not ask for clarification. "This one," he said, pointing to a spotted one that had swum to the front, "is a Texas cichlid. *Herichthys cyanoguttatus*, if you want to get technical. From the family Cichlidae. Actually, all the fish in this tank are cichlids, but there are more than a thousand different species, and new ones are turning up all the time, so I only put a handful of my favorites in here. That one," he continued as another fish, this one speckled with purple, blue and green, darted by, "is a Jack Dempsey."

"Like the boxer?" Clara asked.

"Yep. That's who the species is named after. Because they have kind of a boxer's face, and they can be pretty aggressive in small groups. They're native to Central America—Mexico and Honduras specifically—so they get along well with the Texas cichlid."

The tension between the two of them was ebbing now, allowing Clara to breathe again. She smiled at the image of two fish from opposite sides of the border interacting without incident. Nice to know someone in this room could get along swimmingly. So to speak.

"And that one is called a convict," Grant said, indicating a fish that was black-and-white striped. "For obvious reasons."

"I'm sure he was framed," Clara said, doing her best to lighten the mood further. "He looks too sweet to be a criminal."

Grant identified a half dozen more species as they swam by, offering up snippets about the habits or personalities of each. The more he talked, Clara noted, the more he smiled. And the more he smiled, the more he relaxed. She gradually relaxed, too, until all traces of sexual awareness eased, and she was confident the charged moment they'd shared was only an aberration, never to be repeated.

At least, she was *pretty* confident of that.

As Grant wound down his dissertation on the fish, Clara waited for him to add something that would explain how he came by all his knowledge. But he never did. He only gazed into the aquarium, watching the parade of color. She caught her breath as she watched him, because in that moment, he looked exactly like Hank. Not just the physical resemblance, thanks to the identical genes, but the childlike fascination, too. He looked the same way Hank did when he found a particularly interesting bit of jetsam on the beach. Grown-ups—especially super serious, workaholic grown-ups like Grant—weren't supposed to be distracted by things like colorful fish. Grown-ups were supposed to be worried about stuff like whether or not they were getting enough vitamin D or how they were going to make rent this month.

Well, okay, that was why *some* grown-ups—like, say, Clara—couldn't be distracted by something like colorful fish. Grant hadn't had to worry about making rent his entire life.

"You know, for a guy who sits behind a desk all day," she said, "you sure know a lot about fish. I live just a couple of blocks away from the ocean, and the only thing I know about marine life is which ones are my favorite on any given menu."

He laughed lightly as the two of them straightened, the sound of his voice rippling through Clara like a warm breeze. "Well, that's important to know, too. And these are all freshwater fish. My saltwater aquarium is in my office. It's twice the size of this one, and you'd probably recognize a lot of the guys in there. Clownfish, damselfish, sea horses, grouper..."

"I love grouper," she said. "Grilled, with dill butter on the side."

He chuckled again, and Clara realized the reason she liked the sound of his laughter so much was because she hadn't heard it until now. Frankly, she'd begun to wonder if he was even able to laugh. But the knowledge that he could was actually kind of sobering. If he was able to laugh, why didn't he do it more often?

"You probably love more of them than you realize," he told her. "*Grouper* is a word that applies to fish from several different genera in the *Serranidae* family. There's some sea bass and perch in there, too."

"Wow, you really do know a lot about fish."

For some reason, that made him suddenly look uncomfortable. "It's kind of a hobby," he told her. "Left over from when I was a kid. Back then, I wanted to be a marine biologist and live in the Caribbean when I grew up. Maybe the South Pacific. I even picked out the colleges I wanted to attend. I had this crazy idea as a kid that I could start a nonprofit for research and conservation. My dad even helped me set up a business plan for the thing." He grinned. "I remember I wanted to call it Keep Our Oceans Klean. With a *K*. That way, I could say I worked for a KOOK."

Clara grinned, too. Ah-hah. So, as a child, he *had* wanted to be something specific when he grew up. He *had* had a passion like any normal kid. She was glad for it, even if she wasn't sure why he was sharing that so readily today when, just last night, he'd claimed no memory of such. And she could see him being the kind of kid who would prepare for his college future and make out business plans when most kids were trying to figure out where to go to camp.

"What colleges?" she asked.

He hesitated, and for a minute, she thought he would try to backtrack and tell her he couldn't remember again. Instead, quietly, he said, "College of the Atlantic in Maine for a BS in marine science, then on to Duke for my master's in marine biology. After that, it was a toss-up between University of California Santa Barbara and University of Miami for any postgrad work."

"Why didn't you go?" she asked. "Why didn't you start KOOK? It sounds like a lifelong dream if you're still keeping fish and know so much about them."

Now he looked at her as if she should already know the answer to that question. "There was no way I could do that after my father died."

Clara still didn't understand. For a lot of people, the unexpected death of a loved one made them even more determined to follow their dreams. "Why not?"

Once more, he hesitated. When he finally did speak again, it was in halting sentences, as if the information were being pulled from him unwillingly. "Well… I mean… After my father died, we all… And Brent…"

He halted abruptly, and then tried again. But he was obviously choosing his words carefully. "Brent was actually the one who was supposed to follow in my father's footsteps and run the business after he retired. He was the firstborn, technically, and he seemed to genuinely love the idea of going to work for Dunbarton Industries after he graduated from college. Even when we were little, he used to go in to the office with Dad sometimes, and it wasn't unusual for the two of them to hole up in the office at home in an unofficial Junior Achievement meeting. But after Dad died, Brent…"

He sighed heavily. "Brent reacted to our father's death by regressing. He started shirking responsibility, never did his homework, locked himself up in his room to play for hours on end. Instead of maturing as he aged, he only got more childlike. Even in high school. There was no way he could have gotten into a decent business school with his grades, which was just as well, since he made clear after our father's death that there was no way he was going to take over the company. And Mom wasn't much better. She retreated, too, after Dad died, from just about everything. And she let Brent do whatever he wanted."

It didn't escape Clara's notice that Grant had left himself out of the equation when describing how his family reacted to the death of the Dunbarton patriarch. She could almost see Grant as a child, feeling the same emptiness his mother and brother felt, but not wanting anyone to see him that way.

Before she could stop herself, she asked, "And how

did little Grant react after his father's death? You must have been heartbroken, too."

"I was," he said. "But with my mother retreating and Brent regressing… Someone had to be an adult. Someone had to make sure things got done around here. Mom wouldn't even pay the bills or our employees. The company almost went into receivership at one point. Some of my dad's colleagues stepped in and took over until I could graduate from college and step into the CEO position. So I majored in business and did just that. If I hadn't, the company would have been cut up into little pieces and sold off bit by bit. And then where would the Dunbarton legacy be?"

Clara wanted to reply that the Dunbartons would have made a boatload of money, so their legacy wouldn't be much different from what it was now, and Grant could have followed his dream. But she didn't think he would see it that way. He'd obviously started feeling responsible for his family and the family business when he was still a child himself. Clara got that. She'd assumed responsibility for herself as soon as she understood what responsibility was, and had done the same for Hank as soon as she realized she was pregnant. As a mother, she understood well what it was to put someone else's wants and needs ahead of her own. But she had still pursued her dream of doing something she loved for a living. And if she'd had hundreds of millions of dollars like the Dunbartons did, she'd now have a whole chain of Bread & Buttercream bakeries, and her home office would be in Paris.

"I guess legacies are important," she conceded halfheartedly—mostly because she knew Grant would think that, even if she wasn't quite on board with it herself. "Y'all have had your company for generations and everything. And you want to have something to pass on to your kids someday."

"Oh, I'm not having kids," he told her with conviction.

Too much conviction, really. Grant was only thirty-two. How could he be so sure of something like that? He still had plenty of time.

"Why not?" Clara asked.

Again, he looked at her as if the answer to her question should be obvious. "Because I don't want kids. Or marriage. I don't have time to be a father or husband."

Fair enough, she thought. But… "Then why do you need a legacy? If you're going to be the end of the line, that's even more reason for you to go after your dreams. You could sell the business now, go back to school to major in marine biology and study every ocean on the planet."

Of all the questions she'd asked and observations she'd made, that one seemed to upset him most. "That's not the point," he told her tersely.

"Then what is?"

He waved a hand in the general direction of the aquarium. "The point is that being an aquarist is a hobby. Not a career."

Clara was going to argue with him, since hobbies rarely included knowledge of Latin, never mind use of the word *aquarist*, which she'd sure never used in her life. But he truly did look kind of angry—and not a little distressed—and she didn't want to prolong an exchange that was threatening to become adversarial. So she tried to lighten the mood.

Smiling, she said, "Well. I don't know about you, but I suddenly hope we're having fish for supper."

At first, her attempt at levity seemed to confuse him.

Then it seemed to make him relax. Then he looked kind of grateful that she had relinquished the matter. He even smiled, but it wasn't like the smiles when he was watching his fish, and it never quite reached his eyes. In fact, his eyes were pretty much the opposite of smiling.

"I think it's going to be kebabs," he said. "But we can certainly put in a request for grouper at some point this week. Or next, if you and Hank want to stay a little longer."

Was that an invitation? Clara wondered. Because it kind of sounded like one.

"We can't," she told him. "I don't want Hank to miss too much school, and the bakery will be super busy the closer it gets to Christmas. I just can't afford to stay away any longer," she added when it looked as if he would take exception. "I'm the only full-time baker I have."

But instead of taking exception, he said, "No one would object if you needed to withdraw funds from Hank's trust to help you out with the business. It's there for his needs, but until he's an adult, his needs are joined to yours. If expanding your business and hiring more people would make you more money and increase the quality of Hank's life, then it would be a perfectly acceptable use of the trust."

Clara was shaking her head before he even finished talking. "That's Hank's money," she insisted. "He'll need it for college and for starting his life afterward, whether that's on his own or with someone he loves. Or he'll have it in case of emergency."

"But—"

"I've been taking care of myself and him for a long time, Grant. I've managed fine so far, and I'll continue to manage fine."

"But—"

"You and your mom have been great to both of us, but we'll be heading back to Georgia as scheduled. Thanks, anyway. Now, if you'll excuse me," she continued when he opened his mouth to object again, "there are a couple of things I need to do before supper."

And without waiting for a reply, Clara headed for the door. She assured herself she hadn't lied when she told Grant there were a couple of things she needed to do before dinner. The first was to make sure Hank didn't sleep too long, or he'd be even more insomniac tonight than she was. The second was to remind herself—as many times as it took—that Grant Dunbarton wasn't his brother, and that she needed to stop responding to him as if he were. Because although it hadn't broken her heart when she parted ways with Brent, if she got involved with Grant and then parted ways with him…

She thought again about the happy, childlike look on his face when he was talking about his fish, and the way his expression sobered and grew withdrawn when it came to talking about his work. Well. Something told Clara that if she got involved with Grant and then they parted ways, her heart might never be the same.

As Grant watched Clara leave, he did his best—really, he did—to not stare at her ass. Unfortunately, that was like trying to not breathe. Because the minute his gaze lit on her departing form, his eyes went right to the sway of her hips. And then all he could do was mentally relive that beyond-bizarre moment when he'd been standing behind her by the aquarium, wondering what she'd do if he pulled down her pants, tugged down her panties, freed himself from his trousers and buried himself inside her as deep as he could. Hell, he'd been hard enough to do it, thanks to the expression on her face when he'd looked up from unbuttoning his shirt to find her gazing at him as if she wanted to devour him in one big bite. There was just something about a woman with hungry eyes that made a man's body go straight to sex mode.

Besides, she had a really nice ass.

This was not good. It had been a long time since Grant had been this attracted to a woman this quickly. In fact, he wasn't sure he'd ever been this attracted to a woman this quickly. And the fact that the woman in question was Clara Easton made things more than complicated. He couldn't just have sex with her and then move on. She was going to be a part of his life, however indirectly, for, well, the rest of his life. She would be accompanying Hank to New York whenever he came to visit until the boy was old enough to travel on his own. Hell, she'd be coming to New York with Hank even after he was old enough to travel by himself, because his mother would insist that Clara come, too. She'd also insist Clara and Hank be included in all future holiday gatherings. Hell, knowing his mother, Grant wouldn't be surprised if she convinced Clara and Hank to move into the penthouse at some point. She might even ask Clara to change her name to Dunbarton, too.

Even if none of that did happen, Grant couldn't do the "Yeah, I'll call you" thing with Clara that had always worked well for him in the past, since he was excellent at avoiding women who wanted more than sex and even better at avoiding the ones who wanted a family. After having sex with Clara—who came ready-made with a family—he wouldn't be able to escape seeing her again with some regularity. And *seeing a woman again,* never mind *with some regularity*, was something that wouldn't fit Grant's social calendar.

He wasn't good at relationships. Not family ones, not social ones, not romantic ones. And Clara was threatening to be all three. He couldn't afford responsibilities like that. He had too many other responsibilities. And none of them included other people. Even people who had a great ass. So no more thinking about Clara in any way other than the mundane. Which should be no problem.

All he had to do was make sure he didn't think about her at all.

Five

Grant wasn't surprised when he woke up in the middle of the night. It had taken him forever to get to sleep, thanks to his inability to banish thoughts of Clara from his brain, and he'd slept lightly. Nor was he surprised that when he awoke, it was from a dream about Clara, since he'd still been thinking about her when he finally did go to sleep. He likewise wasn't surprised that the dream had been a damned erotic one, since his last thoughts of her before going to sleep had mostly revolved around her ass. What did surprise him was that he awoke to the smell of cake. Probably chocolate cake. Possibly devil's food cake. Which was easily his favorite.

He glanced at the clock on his nightstand. Three twenty-two. He didn't doubt that there were a number of bakers already up and plying their trade this early in the morning in New York City. However, none of them should have been plying it in the Dunbarton kitchen.

Either someone got seriously lost on their way to work, or Clara was awake, too.

He told himself to go back to sleep. She had said she was an insomniac, so her reasons for being up were probably totally normal and had nothing to do with damned erotic dreams like his. But was it normal for her to be baking at three in the morning? Didn't insomniacs usually just read or watch TV until they fell back asleep?

With a resigned sigh, Grant rose from bed and pulled a white V-neck T-shirt on over his striped pajama bottoms. Then he padded barefoot down the hall toward the kitchen, the smell of cake—oh, yeah, that had to be devil's food—growing stronger with every step. When he finally arrived at his destination, though, he saw not cake, but *cup*cakes, dozens of them, littering the countertops, all with red or green icing. He also saw Christmas cookies and gingerbread men bedecked with everything from gumdrops to crushed peppermint. There were bags of flour and sugar—both granular and powdered—strewn about untidily, as well as broken eggshells and torn butter wrappers, whisks, spoons, spatulas and other things he hadn't even realized they had in the kitchen.

In the middle of it all was Clara, dressed in red flannel pajama pants decorated with snowflakes and an oversize T-shirt bearing the logo for something called the Savannah Sand Gnats. It also bore generous spatters of chocolate and frosting. On her feet were thick socks. Grant had never known a woman who slept in socks. Or flannel. Or something emblazoned with the words *Sand Gnats*. Of course, whenever he was sleeping with a woman, she wasn't wearing anything at all. In spite of that, strangely, there was something about

Clara's socks and frumpy pajamas that was even sexier than no clothes at all.

Her mass of blue-black curls was contained—barely—by a rubber band, but a number of the coils had broken free to dance around her face. Another streak of chocolate decorated one cheek from temple to chin, and when his gaze fell to the ceramic bowl she cradled in the crook of her arm, he saw that it was filled with really rich, really dark chocolate batter, something that meant—*Who's the man?*—the cupcakes in the oven were indeed devil's food.

"Um, Clara?" he said softly.

When she glanced up, she looked as panicked and guilty as she would have had he just caught her helping herself to his mother's jewelry. "Uh, hi," she replied. "What are you doing here?"

"I live here," he reminded her.

"Right," she said, still looking panicked and guilty. "Did I wake you? I'm sorry. I was trying not to make any noise."

"It wasn't the noise. It was the smell. Devil's food, right?"

She nodded. "My favorite."

Of course it was. Because that just made him like her even more. "Were the pecan tarts we had for dessert tonight not to your liking?"

Instead of replying, Clara chuckled.

"What?" he asked.

"Pecan," she repeated, pronouncing it the way he had—the way he always had—*pee*-can. "The way you Northerners say that always makes me laugh."

"Why?"

"Well, first off, because it's wrong."

"No, it isn't."

"Yeah, it is." Before he could object again, she continued, "Look, we Southerners claimed that nut as our own a long time ago, and we say 'pi-*cahn*.' Therefore, that's the correct pronunciation. Also, in case you were wondering, *praline* is pronounced '*prah*-leen,' not '*pray*-leen.' That's another one that really toasts my melbas."

"But—"

"And second of all, I laugh because it always seemed to me like it should be the other way around. Saying 'pi-*cahn*' sounds so hoity-toity, like you Northerners, and saying '*pee*-can' sounds so folksy, like us Southerners." Instead of taking issue with the whole pecan thing—everyone knew the correct pronunciation was "*pee*-can"—he repeated, "So you didn't care for the tarts?"

She started spooning batter into the cupcake pan, an action that delineated the gentle swell of muscles in her upper arms and forearms. Grant wouldn't have thought muscles could be sexy on a woman. But on Clara, muscles were *very* sexy. Then again, on Clara, lederhosen and waders would have been sexy.

"They were delicious," she said. "But I couldn't sleep. And when I get anxious, I bake."

He wanted to ask her what she had to be anxious about. Her son was worth a hundred and forty-two million dollars. She'd never have to be anxious about him—or herself—again. Instead, he asked, "How long have you been up?"

She looked around for a clock. Or maybe she was just gauging the piles of cupcakes and cookies and trying to calculate how long it took to produce that many. "I don't know. What time is it?"

"About three-thirty?"

Now she looked shocked. "Seriously? Wow. I guess I've been up a few hours, then."

She'd been in here for a few hours? Dressed like that? Baking devil's food cupcakes? And he hadn't known it? He was slipping.

In an effort to keep his mind where it needed to be, he focused his attention on the bowl of batter still folded in her arm. Unfortunately, it was way too close to where her T-shirt strained over her torso, offering a tantalizing outline of her breasts and—

"So, what's a Savannah Sand Gnat?" he asked, driving his gaze up to her face again.

"It's our baseball team," she told him as she went back to scooping batter into the cupcake pans.

"Savannah's baseball team is called the Sand Gnats? Seriously?"

She looked up again, narrowing her eyes menacingly. "You got a problem with that?"

"No," he quickly assured her. "But sand gnats aren't exactly endearing, are they? I mean, they might as well have named the team the Savannah Clumps of Kelp."

She shook a chocolate-laden spoon at him. "Don't be dissing my team, mister. I love those guys. So does Hank."

He lifted his hands in surrender. "I apologize. Let me make amends. Dunbarton Industries has a suite at Citi Field. I can take you and Hank to a game someday. Maybe when the Mets play the Atlanta Braves."

And holy crap, did he just invite her to something that was months away and would bring her back to New York for a specific reason to do something with him and not because his mother wanted to see Hank? What the hell was wrong with him?

She dropped the spoon back into the bowl. "See the

Braves play? From a suite? Are you kidding me? Hank would love that."

Grant wanted to ask her if she'd love it, too. Instead he said, "It's a date, then." Crap. Putting it that way was even worse than asking her out in the first place. Quickly, before she could think he meant a *date* date—which he absolutely did not—he added, "For the three of us. Maybe four. Mom doesn't care for baseball, but if Hank is coming, she'll probably want to be there, too."

The comment made Clara's expression go from elated to deflated in a nanosecond. But she said nothing, only went back to furiously spooning the last of the batter into the last cups in the pan, as if wanting to put too fine a point on the whole baking-when-anxious thing.

"Clara?" he asked as she scoured the last bit of chocolate from the bowl. "Is something wrong?"

She didn't look up, only continued wiping the bowl clean, even though she had already scraped it within an inch of its life. Softly, she muttered, "What could possibly be wrong? My three-year-old just became a tycoon. That's every mother's dream, right?"

"I don't know," Grant said. "I'm not a mother. But I would venture a guess that, yes, it would be every mother's dream. You won't have to worry about his future anymore."

At that, Clara did look up. But she no longer looked anxious. Now she looked combative. "I wasn't worried about his future before," she said tersely. "Why would I be?"

Clearly, Grant had hit a nerve, though he had no idea how or why. Clara, however, was quick to enlighten him.

"Look, maybe I've been struggling financially since he was born. Maybe I was struggling financially before he was born. I still manage. I always have. I started a college fund for him as soon as I found out I was pregnant, and I make a deposit into it every month. He's never missed an annual checkup at the pediatrician or twice-yearly trips to the dentist. He gets three nutritious meals a day, clothes and shoes when he needs them, and although Santa may be at the bottom of his toy sack by the time he gets to our apartment, Hank has never had a Christmas morning where he wasn't delighted by his take. No, I can't lay down my platinum card whenever I feel like it and buy him anything he wants, but I give him more love and more time than anyone else ever has, and I will always give him more love and more time than anyone else, and that's way more important than anything a platinum card could buy."

The longer Clara spoke, the more her voice rose in volume and the more vehement she became. By the time she finished, she was nearly shouting. Her eyes were wide, her cheeks were flushed, and her entire body was shaking. When Grant only gazed at her silently in response—since he had no idea how else to respond—she seemed to realize how much she had overreacted, and she slumped forward wearily.

"I'm sorry," she said. She turned around and set the now-empty bowl on the countertop. But instead of turning around again to say more, she only gripped the marble fiercely, as if letting go of it would hurl her into another dimension.

Grant tried to understand—he really did. But the truth was, he had never loved or feared for anyone as much as Clara obviously loved and feared for her son. Grant got how she felt obligated to be the one to provide for Hank. But he didn't understand how she could not be overjoyed about the windfall he had received.

Especially since it could ease significantly all those obligations that could sometimes feel so overwhelming.

As if she'd heard the thought in his head, Clara finally turned slowly to face him. Thankfully, she no longer looked combative. Nor did she look anxious. Now she only looked exhausted.

"I've always been the center of Hank's world," she said quietly, "the same way he's always been the center of mine. Now, suddenly, he has family besides me. He has people to love him and provide for him besides me. And even if they can't love him more than I do, they can provide for him better. There's no way I can deny that. At some point, he's going to realize that, too. If he hasn't already." Her eyes grew damp, but she swiped them dry with the backs of her clenched fists. "There's already a part of me that's afraid he'll want to stay here instead of go home when the time comes for us to go back to Georgia."

Ah. Okay. Now Grant understood. She was afraid of losing her son to his grandmother, because his grandmother was, at this point, pretty much the equivalent of Santa Claus. Actually better than Santa Claus, since Santa evidently arrived at the Easton home having to scrape the bottom of his bag. Grant wished he knew what to say to ease her fears. But the fact was, his mother *could* give Hank anything he wanted, and Clara couldn't. Not that he would ever say that to Clara.

He just wished he did know what to say to her.

He was spared from having to figure it out, however, because the timer went off on the oven, and Clara sprang to grab two oven mitts and remove the pans of cupcakes from inside. Just as deftly, she inserted two more and closed the door, setting the timer again. When she spun back around to face him, she still looked troubled. So much for baking alleviating her anxiety.

"This money from Brent is just going to be so life changing for Hank," she said.

"But it will change his life for the better," Grant told her.

"Will it, though?" she asked. "With so much money comes so much responsibility. And people treat you differently when you have that much money. You treat yourself differently when you have that much money. And I don't want Hank to change."

"Everyone changes, Clara. Change is inevitable."

Without removing the oven mitts—and damned if there wasn't even something about those on her that was sexy—she wrapped her arms around herself, as if physically trying to hold herself together.

"But change should come gradually and naturally," she said. "I don't want Hank to be robbed of a normal childhood or adolescence. I want him to have a childhood where he can go barefoot all summer and catch lightning bugs and put them in a jar with holes punched in the lid and have a lemonade stand on the sidewalk and eat peaches picked right from the tree. I want him to have an adolescence where he works a crappy part-time job and drives a crappy car but loves both because they give him his first taste of freedom. The kind of childhood and adolescence I always wished I had when I was a kid. Hell, I just want Hank to *be* a child and adolescent. I don't want him to grow up too soon. Kids who get thrust into adult positions too early in life..."

When her gaze lit on his, Grant was knocked off-kilter again by just how huge and haunting and bewitching her eyes were. They were even more so when she was so impassioned. He found himself wanting to reach out to her physically, to curl his fingers around her nape and pull her close, and—

"Kids like that," she continued before he could act on his impulse, "kids who are cheated out of a normal childhood, they never grow up to be truly happy, you know? They don't learn how to play as kids, so they never relax or feel joy as adults. They don't make friends as kids, so they never trust or love other people as adults. They just never become the kind of person they might have become if they'd had the same upbringing and chances that regular kids have, and they never stop wondering what kind of person they might have—should have—been, if they'd just been able to grow up at a normal pace. They never stop feeling like, no matter what they have, it's not..." She shrugged, but the gesture was more hopeless than it was careless. "It's not enough."

Grant knew she was talking about herself. He knew everything she said was based on her own experiences growing up, and on her own reality as an adult. He knew she was worried Hank would end up like her. There had been nothing in her monologue that was directed at him, not one thing he should take personally.

For some reason, though, he did take it personally. He took everything she'd said personally. Her comments just struck a chord inside him, too. Discordantly at that. Because although Clara's reasons for being denied a normal childhood were nothing like the reasons he had been denied one, they had both ended up in the same place. That had been made clear at dinner the night before, when both had chorused the same sentiment.

But his life *was* enough, he told himself. Even if, sometimes, it felt as if it wasn't. He wouldn't change a thing about the way he'd grown up, because *his* experiences had made him who and what he was today. And he liked who and what he was. He didn't want to relax—relaxing wasn't in his nature. And he didn't want to love other people—love only complicated otherwise satisfactory relationships. He didn't care if he hadn't grown up to be the person he might have—should have—been, if he'd been allowed to grow up at a normal pace. He liked the person he was just fine. No, not just fine. A lot. He liked the person he was a lot.

But in spite of all his self-assurances, he still sounded defensive when he said, "There's nothing wrong with growing up too soon." Because he said it a little too quickly. A little too tersely. And he couldn't rein it in when he added, "What? Would you rather Hank be like his father and never grow up at all? Spend his life running from one hedonistic adventure to another, leaving before he's done any good, never making a difference anywhere?"

"Of course not," Clara said. "But—"

"At least now Hank has a future," Grant interrupted her. "He can even work in the family business if he wants to. *He* could be the Dunbarton legacy. He could become CEO of Dunbarton Industries after I retire."

Instead of looking pleased, or even intrigued, by the suggestion, Clara looked horrified. "Oh, God, no," she said. "The thought of sweet, happy-go-lucky Hank becoming a joyless, relentless, workaholic CEO who only cares about money is just so…so…"

She shook her head without finishing, obviously unable to find a word abhorrent enough to convey her disgust at the prospect of Hank following in his uncle's footsteps.

She seemed to realize exactly what she'd just said because she immediately told him, "That came out wrong.

I didn't mean *you're* a joyless, relentless, workaholic CEO who only thinks about money. I only meant..."

"Actually, Clara, I think you did mean that," he said.

For some reason, though, Grant couldn't stay angry about the comment. Which could only mean that, on some level, he agreed with it. Not so much that he was joyless. He knew how to enjoy himself. The opportunity for enjoyment just didn't present itself all that often. Nor was he relentless. He could relent under the right circumstances. The need for it just rarely materialized. And he thought about a lot more than money. But money was what kept business in business, and it was as essential to maintaining a quality of life as food and drink were.

So it must be the workaholic part of Clara's accusation that hit home. And, okay, maybe that part was true. Maybe he did work more than the average person did. He had an important job, and it was one no one else in the company could do, because, in spite of its huge size and profits, Dunbarton Industries was still a family business. His position didn't afford time for slacking off. Or, okay, being particularly yielding. Or finding a lot of enjoyment. And it meant he spent a lot of time thinking about the bottom line.

But Clara must understand those things. She was, in effect, the CEO of her own company. Hers was an important job, too, that no one else could do. She must put in longer than usual hours and take work home with her in the form of books to keep and orders to place. She was the last person to be pointing a finger at someone who worked too much at a joyless, relentless job and kept his eye on profitability. She must be as joyless and relentless and profit minded as he was.

But she was doing the thing she had always wanted

to do, he reminded himself, noting the streak of chocolate on her face again…and battling the urge to draw nearer and wipe it—no, lick it—off. She had followed her childhood dream. And she made time for her son. She'd taken off work to bring him to New York to meet the family they hadn't realized he had. Grant thought back on how she'd sat on the floor in Brent's room to play with Hank, and laugh with him, and share an affectionate embrace.

Maybe Clara thought she'd grown up to be unhappy and unfulfilled as a result of being denied a "normal" childhood, but she hadn't. She had learned how to play and to love. Hank had made that possible for her.

So there was really only one joyless, relentless, workaholic CEO who only thought about money in the room. And it wasn't Clara Easton.

She opened her mouth to say something else, but Grant held up a hand to halt her. Nothing she said at this point would ring true. She thought all he did and cared about was work. Which shouldn't have bothered him, since work was pretty much all he did or cared about. It hadn't bothered him when that was his own opinion of himself. But knowing Clara felt that way about him, too…

"Um. Well," he said. "I'll leave you to it."

She hesitated, and then said, "I promise I'll clean up my mess before I go back to bed."

He nodded. "Mrs. Bentley will appreciate that."

"And I'll put some cupcakes and cookies in the freezer, since there are so many. Maybe that will get you and Francesca through Christmas after Hank and I go back to Georgia."

"Mom will appreciate that."

"And you?" she asked.

He looked at her again. "What about me?"

"Will you appreciate them, too?"

He found the question odd. "Of course."

This time Clara was the one to nod. But there was something disingenuous about the gesture. As if she were trying to make him think she believed him, but she really didn't.

"Good night, Clara," he said before turning toward the door again. "I hope you get some sleep."

"Good night, Grant," she replied. Then she said something else he didn't understand. "I hope you get some, too."

Six

The good news was that Clara would have no trouble avoiding Grant the day after calling him a joyless, relentless, workaholic CEO who didn't think about anything but money. The bad news was the reason: as soon as she and Hank had woken up, Francesca announced that the three of them would be spending the day together again, this time at the Bronx Zoo, because Hank loved *Madagascar* so much when he and Francesca watched it together. They might also go to the New York Aquarium if they had time because it had been one of Brent and Grant's favorite places when they were Hank's age.

Although Clara would be able to avoid Grant for the day, she wouldn't be able to avoid him for the morning, since, as she and Hank and Francesca sat in the smaller dining room near the kitchen eating breakfast, Grant joined them.

It quickly became clear that he wasn't exactly happy to see her, either, and wanted to bolt from the house as soon as he could. He was dressed for work in another one of his pinstripe power suits and had his briefcase in hand and a trench coat thrown over one arm. And he barely acknowledged Clara and Hank with a quick "Good morning" before turning to his mother.

"Don't forget you need to look over and okay next year's revised budget before you go out," he told her. "The board is voting on it tomorrow."

Francesca waved a hand airily at her son. "Oh, I'm sure it will be fine. Hank and Clara and I are spending the day together again."

Grant looked surprised by his mother's lack of interest in the corporate budget. "You need to read it, Mom. And you need to be at the meeting to vote on it. We need a quorum, and some of the other board members are—"

"All right, all right," Francesca interrupted him. "I'll read it tonight, I promise. And yes, I'll be at the meeting. Nine o'clock," she said quickly when he opened his mouth, presumably to remind her. Then she looked at Hank and Clara again. "I'll arrange for you and Hank to tour the company while I'm in the meeting tomorrow. It's never too early for a child to learn the ropes of the family business. You could come and work for us someday," she said directly to Hank. "Wouldn't that be fun?"

Clara couldn't help the way her back went up—literally—at Francesca's suggestion. And she could tell that Grant had noticed. Francesca, however, seemed oblivious. As did Hank. At least, he was oblivious to what exactly *coming to work for the Dunbartons* meant, because he jumped on the opportunity faster than a person could say *corporate drone*.

"Okay," he agreed around a mouthful of waffles. "Do you work there, too, Grammy?"

Francesca smiled. "No, but I used to. I was the vice president in charge of public relations before your father and Uncle Grant were born. After that, I helped their father when he was the boss and needed my advice on something. Nowadays, I help the company make money by sitting on the board of directors."

"Are you the boss now?" Hank asked.

"No, sweetheart, your uncle Grant is the boss."

"But you're his mom," Hank objected. "That makes you his boss."

Francesca smiled again and looked at Grant. "Well, in some things, maybe," she said. "But even moms stop being the boss of most things at some point. Uncle Grant is the one who runs Dunbarton Industries." She winked at Grant, and then looked at Hank again. "For now, anyway. But maybe you'll be the boss there someday, Hank. Wouldn't you like that? With your own office and a big desk and lots of people calling you *Mr. Easton*?"

And migraines and chest pains and high blood pressure? Clara thought before she could stop herself. *And no life outside the office whatsoever?*

Grant seemed to know what she was thinking, because although he addressed his next comment to his mother, it was clearly intended for Clara. "Don't push him, Mom. Hank might not want to grow up to be a joyless, relentless, workaholic CEO who only thinks about money. He might want to be a professional beach bum like his father."

Now Francesca threw her son a puzzled look. "What on earth are you talking about? Brent wasn't a beach bum." But she didn't repudiate the first part of Grant's statement.

"Right," Grant said. "Well, then. I'll just head to work to be joyless, relentless and profit obsessed. Have a fun day seeing the sights."

The remark had the desired effect. Clara felt like a complete jerk. She scrambled for something to say or do that might make for a reasonable olive branch. "Grant," she said before he could make his escape. "Don't you want to come with us today? I bet you haven't been to the aquarium in a long time."

He had started to turn away, but halted when she said his name. It was only when he heard the word *aquarium*, though, that he finally turned around.

"It has been a long time," he said. He thought for a minute. "Before my father passed away, in fact."

Clara had figured it had been a while, but even she was surprised to hear it had been decades since he visited a place that must have been a utopia for him when he was a child.

"Then you should take the day off and come with us," she said.

Francesca looked surprised when Clara extended the invitation, but said, "Oh, do come with us, Grant. You loved the aquarium when you were a little boy." Now she looked at Clara. "He would have gone there every day if he could have. I remember there was this one thing he loved more than anything else. We could never pull him away from it. Brent and I could see the entire aquarium in the time Grant took to look at that one thing. What was it called, dear?"

"The chambered nautilus," Grant said in the same tone of voice people used when talking about deities or superheroes. Clara half expected the skies to open and a chorus of angels to break into song.

"That was it," Francesca said to Clara. "I always

thought it was kind of creepy and macabre myself, but Grant was enchanted by it."

"It's a living fossil," he said. "It hasn't changed in four hundred million years. And it lives almost two thousand feet deep and can use jet propulsion to move more than sixty meters per minute. What child wouldn't be enchanted?"

Or what adult? Clara wanted to ask. Since Grant was still obviously enchanted.

"Then you should come with us," Clara said. "You two have been apart for too long."

For one brief, telling moment, Grant's expression changed to the same one that came over Hank whenever Clara took a pan of baklava—his absolute most favorite thing in the world—out of the oven. Then, just as quickly, Grant changed back into businessman mode.

"There's no way I can take today off for that," he said. Though there was something in the way he said it that indicated he really wished he could.

"We could go another day," Clara said. "One you *could* take off."

For a moment, Grant only looked at her in an almost anguished way that seemed to say, *Don't. Just... don't.* But all he said was, "There are no days I could take off for that."

For some reason, Clara just couldn't let it go. "How about Saturday?" she asked. "You don't have to work Saturday, do you?"

His *don't* expression didn't change. "Not at the office, but I'll have plenty to do here."

She opened her mouth again, but he cut her off.

"I can't take time away from work. For anything," he said tersely. Adamantly. Finally.

"Okay," she said. "I just thought maybe—"

"Now if you'll excuse me," he interrupted her, "I have to get to the office. Enjoy the zoo." Almost as an afterthought, he added, "And the aquarium."

And then he was gone, before any of them could say another word. Like "Goodbye," for instance. Or "Have a nice day." Or even "Don't work too hard. Or too relentlessly. Or too joylessly." Though it was clear that Grant Dunbarton didn't have a problem with any of those things.

It was dark when Grant got home from work that night. As it always was this time of year. As it was some days in summer, come to think of it, when he worked especially late. But always, in winter, it was dark. There was a part of him that liked the shorter days. It was quicker to get through them. In summer, when the sun didn't set until eight or nine o'clock, it just felt as if that much more time was wasted somehow. Dark was good. Dark meant night. And night meant the day was almost over.

As he headed through the penthouse toward the stairs, he heard voices coming from the direction of the living room and turned in that direction instead. The room was lit up like, well, a Christmas tree, even though the Christmas tree twinkling in the corner offered the least amount of light. The main illumination came from the two lamps on the tables bookending the sofa, where his mother was sitting reading next year's budget, as she'd promised to do. Although the glass of wine she held and the pajamas and slippers she was wearing seemed incongruous with her reading material, seeing her there reminded Grant of occasions in the past when she'd been more involved with Dunbarton Industries.

She'd always enjoyed working, he remembered, even if she had left the day-to-day operations of the business behind years ago. She still seemed perfectly comfortable now, going over the budget for next year.

On the floor not far from where she sat, Clara and Hank lay on their stomachs with coloring books open before them and crayons littered about. Hank was in his pajamas, too, but Clara was still dressed as she'd been that morning, in khaki cargo pants and a black sweater, her shoes discarded now to reveal socks patterned with images of Santa Claus. Grant smiled at seeing them.

Mother and son were chattering about their individual coloring book creations, Clara saying something about how the jungle animals on her page were conspiring to escape from the zoo, and Hank telling her his had already done that and gone to Madagascar, like in the movie. Clara replied that her animals weren't going to Madagascar. They were going to open a vegetarian café on Fordham Avenue, and that way, they'd be close enough to still visit their animal friends who stayed behind. Hank deemed the plan a solid one, then went back to coloring his own pages, which seemed to consist mostly of jagged lines of, if Grant's Crayola memories served, Electric Lime, Hot Magenta and Laser Lemon. They'd been some of his favorite colors, too, when he was a kid. He was surprised he was able to remember their names so easily. Funny, the things the brain stored that then returned to a person out of nowhere like a surprise birthday present.

"You all look busy," he said as he strode into the room—and wondered when he had decided to do so. His original plan had been to retreat to his office before anyone saw him, the way any self-respecting workaholic CEO would. Not that he was still bothered by Clara's comment or anything. So why was he wading into this patently domestic scene where the only work getting done was by his mother—who tempered her work with wine and did it in her pajamas.

"Hello, dear," his mother said without looking up from the budget. "How was your day?"

He figured he'd played the relentless, joyless workaholic card as much as he could, so he only said, "Fine. Yours?"

"It was lovely," she told him. Finally, she looked up from the budget. "Until I started reading this. There are some huge problems here, you know."

"I know," he said. "That's why I wanted you to look it over before the meeting tomorrow. Have any ideas for where to make improvements?"

"Dozens," she told him. She pointed to the tablet sitting next to her on the sofa. "I'm making notes. Lots of them."

"Good. I've made some, too. We can compare later."

"Uncle Grant!" Hank piped up before Francesca had a chance to reply. "We saw that thing you like so much. At the aquarium. It was awesome!"

Grant smiled. "The chambered nautilus?" he asked. "What did you think of him?"

"I think he winked at me."

Grant chuckled. He'd thought the same thing the first time he saw it, even though that was impossible for the animal. Even so, he told Hank, "That means he likes you. They don't wink for just anyone, you know."

"Really?" Hank asked, sounding genuinely delighted that he had left such an impression.

"Really," Grant assured him. "I bet he's telling all the other cephalopods about you right now, and they're all hoping you'll come back soon to see them." Which was what Grant had always imagined them doing when he was little. He'd completely forgotten about that until Hank mentioned the winking thing. Huh.

Hank looked at Clara. "Can we go back tomorrow, Mama?"

Grant looked at Clara, too, only to find she was already looking at him. And even though her son had asked her a question, she continued to look at Grant. She was smiling at him, too. Smiling in a way that made his heart rate quicken and his blood warm. Not in a sexual way, as usually happened when he looked at her. But in a way that was…something else. Something he wasn't sure he'd ever felt before. Something that almost felt better than sex.

"We can't go back tomorrow, sweetie," Clara told her son. Though she was still looking at Grant and smiling in that…interesting…way. "Grammy wants to show us the place where Uncle Grant works. Where your grandfather used to work. But maybe the next time we come to New York, we can go back."

The next time we come to New York, Grant echoed to himself. How could Clara be talking about leaving already? They'd just gotten here.

Then he remembered they were on day four of their visit. Halfway through the week and a day Clara had said she and Hank could stay in New York. When Gus Fiver had told him and his mother that, Grant had been thinking a week and a day would be more than enough time for an introductory visit. He'd figured all of them would need to take things slowly, that there would have to be a number of such short visits to gradually welcome and include Hank and Clara into the family. But only four days in, Hank and Clara already felt like part of the family. They seemed to be right where they belonged. Their leaving in four days felt wrong somehow.

But they'd be leaving next Monday evening. And who knew when they would make it back?

"Okay," Hank said glumly in response to Clara's promise that they would visit the aquarium on their—admittedly nebulous—return. He went back to his coloring, but his crayon strokes were slower and less enthusiastic than they'd been before.

"Want to join us?" Clara asked.

When she tilted her head toward an assortment of coloring books on the floor that had yet to be opened, it took a moment for Grant to realize her invitation was to lie down beside her and Hank and start filling one in. Yet she had extended the invitation in all seriousness, as if this was the sort of thing people their age did all the time. And, okay, maybe it was something Clara did all the time, being the mother of a three-year-old. It wasn't something Grant did all the time. Or ever. Even if there was something about the idea that sounded kind of fun at the moment.

"Um, thanks," he said. "But I'll pass." Then he couldn't help adding, "It isn't something CEOs do."

"Oh, sure they do," Clara said. She smiled that interesting smile again. "They just color everything the color it's supposed to be and never go outside the lines."

"Very funny," Grant replied dryly. Though, actually, he did kind of find the remark funny.

Ha. He'd show her. He'd lie right down beside her and grab a coloring book and a handful of crayons—Atomic Tangerine, Sunglow and Purple Pizzazz had been other favorites, he recalled—and color all over the damned page, going out of the lines whenever he felt like it, and—

Or, rather, he would do that if he could. If he didn't have so many other things he needed to do. Like go over the budget again so he and his mother could compare notes. Even if he had gone over it twice already. The meeting was tomorrow. He should refresh his memory. Even if he did remember everything pretty well.

"Thanks," he told Clara. "But I have some other things I need to get done before tomorrow."

Because tomorrow was always another day. Another day of things he needed to get done before the next day. Because that day would have things that needed to get done before the day after that. Such was life for a high-powered CEO who didn't have time for things like going to aquariums and coloring zoo animals and having a life outside the office.

"You two have fun," he said to Clara and Hank. To his mother, he added, "I'll be in my office whenever you're ready to go over your proposed changes."

His mother nodded. "Give me another hour or so."

"That's fine," Grant told her. Because that would mean they were an hour closer to the end of the day. An hour closer to bringing on tomorrow. An hour closer to getting done all the important things that needed to get done before other important things took their places.

An hour closer to when Clara Easton would leave New York to return to Georgia.

For the first time in a very long time, Grant was suddenly much less eager to see the day draw to a close.

Seven

By Friday evening, day five of her "vacation," Clara was more exhausted than she was after a full week at her physically demanding, labor-intensive, stress-provoking work, even after sleeping a full five hours later than she normally did on Friday morning. Because the moment she swallowed the last bite of her bagel and the final sip of her coffee, Francesca had hustled her and Hank out of the house to tour Dunbarton Industries' headquarters while she and Grant attended their meeting. Clara had to admit, the tour had been eye-opening and surprisingly interesting. But upon the meeting's conclusion, Francesca had swept the two of them off again, this time to zigzag across Central Park, from the zoo to the carousel to the castle to the Swedish Cottage and its marionettes. Though Clara might just as well have stayed at the penthouse the whole day for all the attention Francesca and Hank had paid her. The majority of her day had been spent catching up with the two of them.

Clara understood. Really, she did. Hank was Francesca's only grandchild, and he was all she had left of Brent. She had a lot of lost time to make up for with him and was trying to squeeze the three and a half years of Hank's life she'd missed into a week's worth of shared experiences that could tide her over until she saw him again. And it was the first time Hank had been the center of someone's universe who never said the word *no*. Yes, he and Clara had plenty of fun together, but there were a lot of times Clara had to tell him no, either because of time or money constraints. Francesca had neither of those, so she was completely at Hank's disposal. And, boy, was he learning that fast.

By the time they returned to the penthouse—after, oh, yeah, dinner at Tavern on the Green—Grant had shut himself up in his office.

Clara grimaced as she thought back on when she'd accused him of being a corporate drone the other night. She hadn't meant to insult him. The words had just popped out. She could hardly be held responsible, because she'd been A) anxious, B) exhausted, C) in the middle of baking enough cookies and cupcakes to feed the United Nations—and their respective nations—and D) trying not to notice how sexy Grant Dunbarton was in a V-neck T-shirt and striped pajama bottoms.

Seriously, when that guy dressed like an ordinary person, he was extraordinarily hot. She was still thinking about just how hot as she sat in the spectacular Dunbarton library to which she had escaped for a little peace and quiet, sipping a glass of luscious pinot noir she hoped would help her forget how hot Grant Dunbarton was. *No!* she immediately corrected herself. The wine would help her relax after yet another day of worrying that her son would abandon her in favor of his grandmother. *No! Not that either!* She was just having a glass of wine to—

Oh, bugger it.

She was having a glass of wine because she really needed a glass of wine—thanks to her growing anxiety over Hank's allegiances *and* her growing attraction to Grant. But where she could pretty much convince herself that Hank would never abandon her, she was less successful convincing herself that her attraction to Grant would go away. Because she was definitely attracted to Grant. Very attracted to him. And the attraction had nothing to do with any misplaced affection for Brent that might still be lingering somewhere inside her. What Clara was feeling for Grant wasn't the breathless infatuation a girl had for a cute guy who was funny and charming and a great kisser. It was… something else. Something she wasn't sure she even wanted to identify, because that could make things even more complicated.

Maybe Clara was only four years older now than she was when she met Brent, but they'd been years filled with mothering and working and trying to build a life for herself and her son. Years of taking on responsibilities and obligations she would have for the rest of her life. The easy, breezy girl who'd fallen for Brent was gone, as were the fast, fun feelings she'd had for him. But the woman who was coming to know and care about Grant? She was another story.

And the last thing Clara needed was to fall for Grant Dunbarton. She shouldn't even find him hot. Sex with him wouldn't be like sex with a guy with whom she'd had no future—precisely because, with Grant, she did have a future. Even if it wasn't a future together, he'd still be in and out of her life thanks to Hank's ties to the family. It was already awkward enough between them. Throwing sex into the mix would only make it more so. Wouldn't it? Of course it would. So she had to keep her distance from the other Dunbarton brother.

"I'm sorry. I didn't know anyone was in here."

As if conjured by her thoughts, Grant spoke from behind her. Clara was so jumpy from both the day and her thoughts that she simultaneously leapt up from the settee and dropped her wine, which crashed into the spectacular Dunbarton coffee table before shattering and sending shards of glass and seemingly gallons of wine—red, of course—falling onto the spectacular Dunbarton Oriental rug.

She cried out at the mess she'd made, then, "Quick!" she shouted at Grant. "I need a towel and some club soda!"

Without questioning the order, he hurried to a bar in the corner of the room and collected the requested items. When he returned, he was already pouring club soda onto the towel and looked even more panicked than Clara was. Damn. The rug must be worth more than she thought.

"Should I call nine-one-one?" he asked.

Well, she didn't think it was worth *that* much.

She grabbed the towel from him, dropping to her knees beside the stain. Grant dropped with her. He wrapped one arm around her shoulders as he withdrew his phone from his pocket. "My God. Are you okay? I'm calling nine-one-one."

"Don't be silly. It's just wine," she said, trying to ignore the heat that seeped through her at the feel of his arm around her shoulder. Why was he doing that? "I can get the stain out, I promise. Or I'll pay to have it professionally cleaned."

He had pressed the nine and the first one, but halted. "You're not bleeding?" he asked. "You didn't fall because you're lightheaded due to blood loss?"

Only then did Clara realize he thought she'd cut herself badly on the broken glass. Meaning his concern wasn't for the rug—it was for her. Which was saying something, because the carpet was massive, stretching from one side of the library to the other, and it could very well have been here since the penthouse was built. It had to be worth a fortune. But he hadn't given it a thought. Some joyless, relentless, workaholic CEO who only thought about money he was.

"I'm fine," she said. She held up her hand for inspection, and realized it was covered with red wine. Hastily, she wiped it off with the towel. "See?" she said, wiggling her fingers to prove it. "Not hurt. Just clumsy."

He took her hand in his and turned it first one way, then the other, just to make sure. Heat shot through Clara from her fingertips to her heart, then seeped outward, into her chest and belly. If she didn't remove her hand from his soon, that heat was going to spread even farther, right down to her—

Oops. Too late.

She tugged her hand free and went back to work on the stain. But Grant circled her wrist with sure fingers again and drew her hand away. Once more, Clara was flooded with sensations she hadn't felt for a long time. Too long. She'd honestly forgotten how nice it could be, just the simple touch of a man's bare skin against her own.

"There could be broken glass in there," he said from what sounded like a very great distance. "I'll call someone tomorrow to have the rug cleaned professionally. Until then, we can close off the room to make sure Hank doesn't wander in here."

"But—"

"It's okay. Really. We don't use this room that often anyway."

"You were about to use it tonight," Clara pointed out.

"No, I wasn't. I just came in to fix a drink." He smiled. "The good bourbon is in the library."

She smiled back. "Right. All that stuff in the kitchen pantry must be complete rotgut."

His smile grew, reaching all the way to his eyes, and the bubbling heat in Clara's torso bubbled higher. "We only keep that for the servants, so they'll have something for when we drive them to drink."

So much for his being humorless, Clara thought. When he put his mind to it, Grant could be every bit as funny and charming as his brother. Though he was being a bit relentless about not letting go of her wrist. Not that she really minded, even though she should.

"But club soda is amazing," she objected halfheartedly, trying to focus on something other than the gentle feel of his warm fingers around her wrist. "It'll work. I swear."

He didn't reply, but didn't let go of her hand, either. In fact, he ran his thumb lightly over the tender flesh on the inside of her wrist, making her pulse leap wildly. Something he probably felt, since his thumb stilled on her skin right about where her pulse would be. He continued to watch her intently, his lips parted, his eyes dark. For one tiny moment, Clara thought he might actually lean in to kiss her. For one tiny moment, she really wished he would. Then, suddenly, he freed her wrist and reached for the towel in her other hand, pressing it carefully into the stain.

"Club soda is good for stains, is it?" he asked as he worked. He picked up pieces of glass where he found them, setting them on the coffee table.

Clara nodded. Then, realizing he couldn't see the gesture, because he was still dabbing at the rug and picking up glass, she said, "Uh-uh." Mostly because that was the only sound she could manage.

"Spill wine a lot, do you?" he asked, smiling again, more softly this time. But he still didn't look at her as he continued to work on the stain.

"Well, not as often as juice," she said, "which club soda also works great on. But I am a harried mother of a toddler, so there are days when wine is one of the four basic food groups."

"They don't use the four basic food groups anymore," he said. Still cleaning up her mess. Still smiling. "It's the food pyramid now."

"Actually, that's been replaced, too," she told him. "By something called MyPlate. Which is pretty much the four basic food groups again, except they separated fruits and vegetables, and they put dairy in a cup."

Having evidently decided he'd done as much as he could to control the damage, Grant looked at Clara again. But his eyes were still dark, and his mouth was still much too sexy for her well-being. "So what are the four basic food groups of the harried toddler mother?" he asked.

Clara was tempted to say merlot, Chardonnay, pinot grigio and Cabernet, but stopped herself. She almost never drank pinot grigio. So she said, "Smoothies, whatever's left on the toddler's plate when he's done eating, Lärabars and wine."

Grant nodded. And still looked as though he might kiss her.

So she said, "Really, just give me ten minutes and I can have this rug looking good as new."

"You'll have your work cut out for you," he told her. "It's more than a hundred years old."

Clara closed her eyes. "Wow. That so doesn't make me feel better."

He chuckled at that. "It should. Can you imagine how much stuff has been spilled on this rug in that length of time? In my lifetime alone? Brent and I weren't exactly clean kids."

His expression cleared some at the mention of his brother, and Clara was grateful for the change. He picked up a few more pieces of glass and gave the rug a few more perfunctory pats, then left the towel over the stain to alert any unsuspecting library visitor of its presence. Then he rose from the floor and held out a hand to help up Clara. But she pretended she didn't see it and stood on her own.

"'Clean kids' is an oxymoron," she said when they were both vertical again. "I can't imagine having two of them underfoot at the same time. Francesca must have had her hands full with the two of you."

Grant smiled again. "Yeah, well, I think the fact that she and my father never had any more kids after the two of us speaks volumes."

Clara waited for his expression to cloud over again at the realization that he was the only Dunbarton child left. Instead, he still seemed to be steeped in fond nostalgia for their childhood. He looked past Clara, gesturing at a chair near the fireplace.

"I remember once, my dad was sitting over there reading an annual report when Brent and I came tear-ing through here. I don't remember which one of us was chasing the other. Maybe we were racing or something. Anyway, my dad was also enjoying what was probably some ridiculously expensive brandy—he did love his Armagnac—and Brent knocked it off the table and onto the hearth. Broke the snifter into bits, which probably added another couple hundred bucks to the damage. Then he tried to pass himself off as me, so I'd have to take the blame."

"You don't sound too mad about that."

Grant shrugged. "It was only fair. I'd passed myself off as him at school the week before when I got caught in the halls during class without a hall pass. Problem was the teachers really did have a tough time telling us apart. But Mom and Dad never did. Brent had to pay for that snifter out of his allowance. But I paid for half. Least I could do."

Now Clara chuckled. "Did you guys do that often? Pretend to be each other?"

Grant smiled again. "Only when we were absolutely sure we could get away with it."

She could believe that about Brent, mischievous guy that he was. But she was having a hard time imagining Grant as the naughty child.

"Come on," he said, tilting his head toward the bar. "I'll pour you another glass of wine. There's a really nice Harlan Estate in the rack. So much better than that rotgut from the pantry."

She was about to tell him the rotgut in their pantry cost about five times what she had in her own pantry, but halted. Who was she to turn up her nose at a really nice Harlan Estate?

He opened a bottle and poured them each a generous serving of dark red wine. He handed one glass to

Clara and then, almost as an afterthought, picked up the bottle to take it with them.

"Is Mom with Hank?"

Clara nodded, her stomach knotting with anxiety again. This was the first time Hank had spent more of his day with someone else than with Clara. For his first two years, he'd stayed in the bakery with her, playing in a part of the kitchen the then-owner had childproofed for him. Everyone who worked there had looked after him. When he'd started preschool at two, he'd still spent the bulk of his day with Clara at the bakery. Since coming to New York, though, Francesca had clocked more time with him than Clara had. And Clara still wasn't quite okay with that. But she couldn't bring herself to deny Francesca all the time with Hank she wanted, knowing it would be months before they could come back to New York for a visit.

"The marionette show was 'Jack and the Beanstalk,'" Clara said. "Francesca told Hank it was his father's favorite book when y'all were kids, and promised to read it to him when we got ho— Ah, back to the penthouse."

After mentioning his brother, Clara waited to see if Grant would revisit memories of his childhood again, but he only said, "The living room, then. It will be quiet in there." He hesitated for a moment before adding, "You look like you could use some quiet."

Was it that obvious? But all she said was, "Thanks. Some quiet would be good."

The Dunbarton living room was even more spectacular than the Dunbarton library, with its veritable wall of windows on one side looking out on the nighttime skyline and a dazzling blue spruce trimmed with glittering decorations and seemingly thousands of twinkling lights. The furnishings were elegant and tailored, the color of luscious gemstones, and the walls were painted a deep, rich ruby. The only other illumination in the room came from a fire someone had set in the fireplace, warmly crackling in invitation, and a half dozen candles in a candelabrum placed on the center of the mantelpiece amid pine boughs and holly berries.

Grant must have seen how her gaze lingered there, because he told her, “Mrs. Weston always lights the place up before she retires for the day. And then we just let the fire burn itself out.”

Clara marveled again at the lifestyle the Dunbartons enjoyed. The lifestyle Hank might enjoy someday, if he wanted. She just couldn’t jibe the life he’d led so far with the one that awaited him. Every year it was going to be harder to tear him away from this and get him to return to their modest life in Georgia. Living here was like living in a Hallmark Christmas card, Clara thought. Until she sat down on the sofa and noticed there wasn’t a single present under the tree.

“Someone needs to start shopping,” she said. “There are only twenty-two shopping days left until Christmas.”

Grant smiled as he placed the bottle of wine on the end table beside him. “No worries. We stopped exchanging gifts years ago. Bonuses for the servants, doormen and concierge, but that’s about it.”

“You and Francesca don’t exchange gifts?”

He seemed to find the question odd. “No.”

Maybe when people reached a certain income bracket where they didn’t really need anything anymore, they stopped buying Christmas presents for each other. Clara supposed it was possible. But it seemed unlikely. There was more to Christmas than getting stuff, and there was more to gift giving than simply supplying someone with an essential item—or even a luxury.

Gifts under a Christmas tree weren't meant to replace love and attention. They were meant to symbolize it. That was why even the poorest families struggled to put *some*thing under the tree. To show the other members that they were important and cherished. To find an empty Christmas tree in a home like the Dunbartons', who should find gift giving effortless and enjoyable, was just… Well, it was kind of heartbreaking, truth be told.

"Why not?" she asked. She told herself she should just let it go. It was none of her business why Grant and Francesca didn't exchange gifts. For some reason, it just bothered her that they didn't. A lot.

But he didn't seem bothered at all. He just shrugged and said, "I don't know. We just don't. We haven't since…" He thought for a minute, clearly not able to even remember when the tradition came to a halt. "I guess since Brent left home. He always bought gifts for me and Mom, so we always got him something. After he left, we just…didn't do it anymore."

Meaning that, if it hadn't been for Brent, they would have stopped even before then.

"But there should always be gifts under a Christmas tree," Clara objected. "Even if there are only a few. It's naked without them."

Grant didn't seem to take offense. "Okay. I'll tell the service who decorates for us that next year, they should wrap some boxes and put them under the tree when they finishing decorating it to add to the holiday mood."

Clara gaped at that. "You don't even put up your own Christmas tree?"

He shook his head. "Mom hires a service to do that every year."

Clara gaped wider. "There are people who get paid to put up other people's Christmas trees?"

"Sure. And the wreaths and the garlands and everything else." When he finally realized how appalled she was by the concept of a Christmas-for-hire, he added, "I mean, they do use our stuff. We're not renting from them the way a lot of people do."

"People *rent* their Christmas?" Clara asked, outraged. Why bother decorating at all if you weren't going to do it yourself?

Instead of being offended by her tone, Grant just shrugged again. "Welcome to the twenty-first century, Clara. And to New York City. A lot of people like to have their houses decorated because they entertain friends or clients. But they don't want the hassle of doing it themselves."

"But putting up the tree is the best part of Christmas. Well, after opening presents, at least." Then she thought about that some more. "No, it is the best part. It still feels Christmassy before and after the presents are opened. But it can't feel Christmassy without a tree."

"I bet Hank's favorite part is the presents."

Clara shook her head. "Oh, don't get me wrong. He loves the loot. But that part only lasts one day. The tree stays up for a month. And decorating it is easily the funnest thing of all. Don't you miss that part?"

"What part?"

"How every year, when you take out the ornaments, you remember some of them you forgot you had, and then you remember where you got them and what you were doing then and how much has changed. Putting up a Christmas tree is like revisiting your whole life every year."

Grant looked dubious. "Correct me if I'm wrong, but you and Hank have only had…what? Four Christmases together?"

"But even before Hank," she said, "I always put up a tree, starting with my freshman year in college. My dorm mates and I pooled our funds and bought a tree, and we found ornaments at thrift shops and discount stores. We split them up after we graduated. I still have mine," she added. "And when I put them on our tree every year, I remember those dorm mates and being in college, and that first breath of freedom where I could do anything I wanted without permission." She smiled. "Like put up a Christmas tree in my own place, with my own stuff, and if I fell in love with one of the ornaments, no one could say it didn't belong to me so I couldn't take it with me when I went to live somewhere else."

Grant had been smiling while she talked, but he sobered at that. "Did that happen to you?"

She hesitated, wondering why she had even brought the incident up. Wondering, too, why it still hurt nearly twenty years after the fact. "Yeah," she said softly. "When I was eight. Looking back, the ornament wasn't all that great, really. A little plastic Rudolph with a broken leg whose red nose had been rubbed white over the years. I painted him a new one with some red nail polish, and I glued his leg back on with way more glue than was necessary, so it left a gigantic lump. Then I put him back on the tree and admired him every day. I don't know why I loved him so much. I guess I felt kind of responsible for him or something. I was moved to a new place the week before Christmas that year, and

I wanted so badly to take him with me. But my foster mother said no."

"Why?"

This time Clara was the one to shrug. "I don't know. She didn't say. A lot of questions I asked back then never got answered, though. It wasn't unusual."

He looked as if he wanted to say something else, but instead, he only gazed at her in silence. Long enough that the air around them began to grow warm. Long enough that she thought again he might kiss her. Long enough that she wished he would.

"Um, I should go check on Hank and Francesca," she said. "If he likes a story enough, he wants it read over and over again, and it can get kind of annoying."

She stood before Grant had a chance to say anything and hurried out of the living room. Only after she was heading down the hall toward Hank's room—she meant Brent's old room—did she realize she hadn't even tasted the glass of wine Grant had poured for her.

Eight

Grant went into the office the day after his and Clara's heart-to-heart by the Christmas tree, even though it was a Saturday. Not because he had a lot of things to do he hadn't finished during the week. On the contrary, things slowed down a lot between Thanksgiving and New Year's. He just figured he would take advantage of the weekend to catch up on some email and other things. It had nothing to do with how he wanted to avoid Clara, because she might still look the way she had last night. Not just when she'd shown her distress that the Dunbartons didn't do Christmas the traditional way. But when she told him about the Rudolph ornament at her old foster home. She might as well have been eight years old again, being shuttled to a new, strange place, so lost and lonely had she seemed in that moment.

Once he arrived home, Grant still wanted to avoid her, and for the same reasons. He sighed as he tossed his briefcase onto his bed and then went about the motions of undressing. After slipping into a pair of dark wash jeans and a coffee-colored sweater, he headed to the library for a bourbon. The rug cleaners had already come and gone, and the carpet looked good as new again. Well, okay, good as a hundred years old again. He poured a couple of fingers of Woodford Reserve into a cut crystal tumbler and headed out to the living room. It, too, looked exactly as it had the night before, minus Clara, a glaring absence that made the whole room seem off somehow. He was about to turn and make his way somewhere else, somewhere that wasn't so quiet, when his gaze lit on something that hadn't been in the room the night before—four gifts under the Christmas tree, each wrapped in a different color of foil paper, topped with curly ribbon.

Although he was sure he knew who had left them there, he couldn't help moving to the tree for a closer look. When he stooped, he saw that each bore a tag and that two were for him and two were for his mother. The larger ones were from Clara, the smaller ones were from Hank. Not that Grant thought for a moment that Hank had shopped and paid for them. But he wouldn't be surprised if Clara had asked the boy for final approval.

He set his drink on the floor and reached for the gift that was addressed to him from Clara. It was cube-shaped, large enough to hold a basketball and heavy. Unable to help himself, he gave it a gentle shake. Nothing. Whatever was in there, she'd packed it well enough to keep it from moving. He replaced it and lifted the one to him from Hank. It was square and flat and much lighter. But it, too, was silent when he gave it a shake. He set it next to the other one, palmed his drink and stood.

Damn. Should he give gifts to them in return? Not that Grant minded giving gifts. He just didn't want to brave the crowds to shop for them. Especially since he had no idea what to get a three-year-old boy. Or Clara, for that matter. The only time he'd bought gifts for women, they were to make up for some oversight. A date he'd forgotten, a wrong word at the wrong time, taking too long to return a call, something like that. He generally bought jewelry, because that was always a safe bet with women. At least, it was for the women he dated. Clara, though… For one thing, she didn't seem to wear much jewelry. For another, jewelry seemed like the kind of thing you gave a woman when you didn't know what else to get her. It was his go-to gift because he'd never wanted to work that hard to figure a woman out. Clara, though…

Clara. For some reason, he did want to figure her out. He just had no idea how to go about it. And he couldn't help thinking it would be a bad idea to try. Because the more he'd learned about her over the past few days, the more he'd liked her. And the more he'd wanted to learn. And he just couldn't risk getting involved with her, not when he wouldn't be able to make a clean break after whatever happened between them came to an end.

Because it would come to an end. It always came to an end. Grant wasn't the kind of man to make a long-term commitment to a woman. Not when he already had a long-term commitment to his work. Besides, in spite of the undeniable attraction he and Clara felt for each other, they weren't well suited. She'd made clear she wanted what she considered a "real" life for her son, one in her small town, surrounded by simple pleasures. She wanted to temper her work with play and her reality with dreams and her sense with sensibility. And that just wasn't Grant's way. At all.

Sure, they could potentially engage in a sexual liaison. Sure, it could potentially be incredible. But it wouldn't last. He was sure of that, too. He and Clara were too different from each other, and they both wanted entirely different things from life. Getting involved with each other would only make life more difficult for them both when their paths inevitably—and regularly—crossed in the future.

The living room, like the library, was too quiet. The whole house was too quiet. Where was everybody?

He wandered into the kitchen to find it empty, though there were signs someone had been snacking in here not long ago. There were cookie crumbs on the counter, and an empty milk glass in the sink. Suddenly, he heard laughter that sounded as if it was coming from the dining room. He headed in that direction and found Clara and Hank lying on the floor on the other side of the expansive table, gazing up at the planets on the ceiling. Clara was pointing at one of them, and Hank was still laughing at something one of them must have said.

Neither of them had seen or heard him come in, so Grant stood still and silent in the doorway, watching them. Hank was already in his pajamas, blue ones dotted with some cartoon character Grant had never seen, and Clara was in a pale green sweater and blue jeans. But the sweater was cropped at the waist, and riding higher because of the position of her arm, revealing a tantalizing bit of naked torso between its hem and the waistband of her jeans. Grant did his best not to notice how— Oh, hell, no he didn't. He zoomed right in on the milky skin and wondered if it felt as soft as it looked.

"No, not Plu-*toad*," Clara said, sending Hank into

another fit of giggles. "Plu-*toh*." But she was laughing, too, by the time she finished.

"I think it should be Plu-toad," Hank said. "And only frogs should live there."

"You know, Hank" Grant said, "frogs and toads aren't the same thing."

Both Hank and Clara scrambled up off the floor as if it had caught fire, looking guiltily at each other before turning to Grant.

"Don't worry," he hurried to tell them. "I used to lie in here looking at that ceiling all the time. Go back to what you were doing."

"That's okay," Clara said. "We were finished."

"Anyway," Grant said to Hank, "If you want frogs to live there, you should call it Plu-frog."

That made the boy giggle again, which gave Grant an odd sense of satisfaction. He didn't recall having put *Make a child laugh* on his bucket list, but now that he'd accomplished the feat, it seemed like something everyone should attempt at least once. It felt kind of good, having done it.

When it seemed as if none of them was going to ever speak again, Grant said, "So I noticed someone left some presents under the Christmas tree today."

"We did!" Hank cried. "Mama and me went out this morning and—"

Clara clamped a gentle hand over her son's mouth and shot him a meaningful look. "And got coffee," she finished for him. "Right, sweetie?"

Hank hesitated, and then nodded vigorously, so she removed her hand. "Right," he agreed. "Mama got coffee, and I got hot chocolate. And then we didn't—"

Clara clamped her hand over his mouth again. "We have no idea how those gifts got under the tree."

"Funny," Grant said, "the tags said they were from you and Hank."

Clara and her son exchanged another look, this one full of comical wide-eyed innocence. Then they both shook their heads in exactly the same way and stretched out their arms in identical comical shrugs. Then they looked at Grant again.

"No clue," Clara said.

"No clue," Hank echoed.

"Then I guess it would be okay if I open mine now?" Grant asked.

Clara shook her head. "No, that would not be okay. You have to wait until Christmas morning, just like everyone else."

"I can't even open it Christmas Eve?" he asked.

"Don't worry, Uncle Grant," Hank said. "Mama never lets me open my presents till Christmas morning, either." He threw his mother a chastising look as he added, "Even though *all* my friends get to open one on Christmas Eve."

"Oh, and if all your friends jumped off a bridge, would you do that, too?" Clara asked him.

"Maybe," Hank told her. "If it was on Plu-toad!" He punctuated the statement with a childish laugh. Clearly this was high humor for three-year-olds.

Actually, Grant wanted to laugh, too, but Clara gave her son a stern look that silenced them both…until she groaned and started laughing, too. Then the three of them made a few more jokes about Plu-toad, until the humor just became so weird, only a three-year-old—or a couple of especially silly adults—could understand it.

"Enough," Clara finally said to her son with one last breathless chuckle. "You're never going to get to sleep tonight. Go brush your teeth and tell Grammy good-night. If she doesn't have time to read you a story, I can. But bedtime is in thirty minutes!" she called after him as he scampered off. "I mean it, Hank!"

She looked exhausted when she turned back to Grant. "He's been sneaking out of his room…I mean, Brent's room…after bedtime to watch TV with your mother. He's fallen in love with *Oliver and Company*, which is probably one of the movies Disney just stuck back in the vault, so I won't be able to find it on Tybee Island, or it will cost a fortune on eBay, so I won't be able to afford it, which is just one more way your mother will lure us back here. I don't know which one of them I want to ground more."

Grant smiled. "Take away her Bergdorf's card for a week. That'll teach her."

Instead of laughing, Clara sat down on the floor and lay back again to gaze up at the ceiling. Not sure what made him do it—maybe it was the way her sweater rode up again—Grant lay down beside her.

And looked up at the star- and planet-studded ceiling from that vantage point for the first time in twenty years. Wow. He'd forgotten how much cooler it was from this angle. He really could almost pretend he was lying in a field out in the middle of nowhere, the way he had done when he was a child.

"We have to go home in two days," Clara said abruptly.

The comment surprised him, even though she wasn't telling him anything he didn't already know. Somehow, it just felt as if she and Hank had been here for months. It felt as if they should be here for more months. Surprising, too, was how melancholy she sounded about going home. She'd made no secret of her fear that Hank wouldn't want to leave after spending time with his grandmother. Grant would have thought Clara would be relieved to be going home in a few days. Of course, he thought he'd be relieved about that, too, since it meant he would stop entertaining such ridiculous ideas about the two of them. But he didn't feel any more relieved than she sounded.

"Maybe you can come back after the holidays," he said, intending the comment to be casual and perfunctory. Realizing after he said it that it was actually serious and hopeful.

She said nothing at first, just looked up at the stars. Then she turned her head to look at him full on. She was so close. And her eyes were so green. Her black curls were piled on the floor, scant inches away, close enough for him to reach over and wind one around his finger. Would it be as silky as it looked? It was all Grant could do not to find out for himself.

"It's going to break Hank's heart to leave," she said. "He's fallen in love with your mother, and she's been so wonderful with him. And between his school and my work, it's going to be summer before we can get back for a visit."

"What about spring break?"

She shook her head. "Too close to Easter. It's super busy at the bakery then. No way could I take the time off. Especially after taking this week at Christmastime."

"Then Mom can come visit Hank in Georgia."

Clara looked fairly panicked at that.

"Is that a problem?" he asked.

"Well, our apartment is just so small. There's only the two bedrooms. And only one bathroom. No way would Francesca be comfortable staying with us."

Grant smiled. Of course Clara would assume that family would want to stay with, well, family. "She'd stay in a hotel, Clara. They do have hotels on Tybee Island, I assume?"

Clara nodded earnestly, thinking he was serious about asking if there were hotels in a popular seaside destination.

"She'd probably prefer that, anyway," he said. "She does like her room service."

For some reason, that made Clara look even more panicked. "Hank might want to stay with her at the hotel. He loves hotels. We hardly ever get to stay in one. Especially the kind that have room service. He'd be thrilled."

"Then his staying with Mom would give you some time to yourself. Surely, it would be nice to have a break."

She sighed and looked at the ceiling again. "Yeah."

Funny, she didn't sound as if she thought it would be nice.

She was still worried about losing Hank to the Dunbarton lifestyle. Still worried his mother would take her place in Hank's heart. Which was crazy because, number one, no child who had a relationship like Hank clearly did with Clara would put anyone else before his mother. And number two—

Number two, Grant really, really wanted to tangle his fingers in her hair and trace the elegant line of her jaw with his fingertip, and then, when she looked at him again, roll toward her and cover her mouth with his, and then cover her body with his, and then—

"Breaks are good, right?" she said softly. She was still gazing at the stars overhead, but she seemed to be seeing something else entirely.

It took him a minute to rewind to the point in the conversation when they'd been talking about his mother visiting her and Hank in Georgia. But even when he remembered, the thought fell by the wayside, because he was still too focused on one strand of hair that had stayed pressed against her cheek when she turned her head to look back up at the ceiling.

Without thinking about what he was doing, he reached across the few inches separating them and tucked a finger beneath the sable curl. He told himself it was just to free it from her skin—her luscious, glorious skin—since hair stuck in place like that could be pretty damned annoying. But his gesture left the back of his knuckle pressed against her cheek—her luscious, glorious cheek—and the moment he realized her skin was indeed as soft as it looked, he couldn't quite pull his hand away again. Instead, he grazed his finger lightly along the elegant line of her jaw, once, twice, three times, four, even after the strand of hair had fallen away.

At first, he thought he must be touching her so lightly that Clara didn't even notice he was doing it. Then he glimpsed a hint of pink blooming on her cheek and noted how the pulse at the base of her neck leaped higher. Her lips parted softly, and her chest rose and fell with her more rapid respiration. Grant noted then how his own breathing had hitched higher, how his own heart was racing and how heat was percolating beneath his own skin, too. When she turned her head again to look at him, her pupils were expanded, her cheeks were ruddy and her lips parted wider, as if she would absolutely welcome whatever he wanted to do. And what Grant wanted to do in that moment, what he wanted more than anything in the world, what he wanted more than he'd ever wanted anything in his life was to…

Slowly, he pulled his hand away from her face and settled it on his chest. "Your hair," he said, having to push the words out of his mouth as if they were two-ton boulders. "It…it was caught on your, um…your cheek."

Clara continued to gaze at him in silence, looking as if she couldn't remember any better than he did where they were or what they were supposed to be doing.

He tried again. "I just wanted to, um… I know how damned annoying that can be."

She nodded slowly, but said nothing for another charged moment. Then, softly, she told him, "Thanks. Yeah. I hate when that happens."

But she didn't stop staring at him. And she didn't stop looking sensuous and desirable and hot as hell. And he didn't stop wanting to…

He had to stop thinking about her this way. It really was ridiculous, his pointless preoccupation with Clara. He should be happy she was leaving in a few days. After she was gone, he could go back to being preoccupied with other things. Things that were actually important. Like work. And also work. And then there was work. And he couldn't forget about work. All of which were really important, something he wished Clara could understand. Maybe if she realized just how important his work was, she wouldn't be so quick to dismiss a position at Dunbarton Industries, working toward CEO, as a possible future for Hank. Who knew? Maybe the boy would end up being more like his mother than his father and actually enjoy running a business. Just because it might not be the business he originally wanted to run… Just because it wasn't, say, Keep Our Oceans Klean… Hank could adapt.

"It's good that you're here now, though," Grant told her. "And you know, it just occurred to me that the company holiday party is tomorrow night."

Which actually hadn't just occurred to him. He'd

known it was on his schedule for some time. And he'd thought about asking Clara if she wanted to come, but had decided she wouldn't want to because of her less than warm and fuzzy feelings about the corporate world. Suddenly, though, for some reason, inviting her seemed like a really good idea. For Hank's sake. Not for Grant's.

"It's a family friendly event," he added. "We encourage all of our employees to bring their spouses and kids. I'm sorry I didn't invite you before now. I wasn't sure you'd be interested. Mom and I go every year. Kind of necessary for us, me being the boss and her being on the board of directors. But you and Hank should come this year, too. You can see what Dunbarton Industries is really all about."

"You mean I can see what Hank's legacy could be," she amended.

"Okay, that, too," he admitted. "Maybe you'll see that it's not as joyless and relentless as you think."

She sighed softly, meeting his gaze earnestly now, something that somehow made her seem even more accessible than her heated looks had a moment ago. Something that somehow doubled his desire to reach for her.

He really, really had to stop thinking stuff like that.

"I truly am sorry about saying that, Grant. I didn't mean I thought you were like that."

Yeah, she did. But maybe her coming to the party would change her mind. Instead of saying that, though, he only said, "Apology accepted." Then, because she still hadn't accepted—or declined—his invitation, he asked, "So do you and Hank want to come to the holiday party with me and Mom?"

She hesitated only a moment—but it was still a moment, which was telling in itself—then replied, "Sure.

Why not? It's probably the only holiday party I'll get to attend this year. With grown-ups, anyway. I'm going to be swamped at the bakery after we get back." Then she smiled, and her distress seemed to evaporate. "Thanks for inviting us, Grant."

She was thanking him? For what? He was the one who had just received a gift in the form of her acceptance. And it was the nicest gift he'd received in years.

"It'll be fun," he told her. Which was something he always automatically said about the Dunbarton holiday party, even though he never meant it. This year, he did mean it. And for that, he was grateful to Clara Easton, too.

Okay, so the corporate headquarters of Dunbarton Industries wasn't as sterile and soul-sucking as Clara had assumed it would be before her first visit here with Francesca. So the main offices looked as if they'd been designed by Frank Lloyd Wright, with open spaces, organic lines, satiny woodwork and sleek Prairie School furnishings. So Grant made sure that a sizeable chunk of the company's profits went toward making its employees more comfortable and happier in their work environment. She still couldn't see Hank working here someday.

But then, she couldn't really see Grant working here today. As nice as the place was, and as upright, forthright and do-right as he was, he still seemed out of place here, even after having helmed the corporation for nearly a decade, and even though his employees clearly liked him. Francesca, yes, Clara thought. She was totally at home here, not just amid the polished, sophisticated surroundings, but also in flitting from one person to another, saying hello and chattering about their work and their families and ensuring that everyone was happy at their jobs in general and having a good time this evening. But Grant?

Although he, too, had spent much of the evening moving from one person to another to speak to them all, there had been no flitting or chattering on his part. He'd seemed reserved without being standoffish, serious without being stodgy and businesslike without being self-important. Which, okay, were all good traits for a boss to have.

He still seemed out of place here.

And Clara felt out of place, too, even having been here twice now. She just wasn't used to being in a workplace that was so...clean. Her professional environment was always scattered with utensils and dusted with flour and sugar. Stains in a rainbow of colors were an integral part of any shift. By the end of her workday, there was confectionary chaos to clean up, and she was a sticky mess. And she liked it that way. All of it.

She would never go into her workplace dressed as she had for the party tonight, in a formfitting, claret-colored, off-the-shoulder velvet cocktail dress and pearl necklace and earrings—even if they were faux. And black stilettos? Uh-uh. Not unless she wanted to break her neck on some spilled pastilles or frosting.

Grant, however, wore another one of his dark power suits and looked perfectly normal—if not quite comfortable—in it. His only nods to festivity were in his necktie—one that was dark red and spattered with tiny bits of holly—and a small boutonniere of evergreen and berries that his mother had affixed to his lapel before they left the penthouse.

He'd been much less restrained with the office decorations—or, at least, whomever he'd put in charge of decorating had been, but they'd obviously met with his approval. Everywhere Clara looked, she saw signs of the season. A giant Christmas tree in the corner was lit up like, well, a Christmas tree. A shiny silver menorah was ready for lighting when Hanukkah began. Not far from it was set up an mkeka for Kwanzaa, along with a kinara set to be lit the day after Christmas. She'd learned a lot about Kwanzaa as the room mom planning the holiday party for Hank's class last year and through orders at the bakery. And the oversize ice bucket with the magnum of champagne had to be for New Year's. Someone had even installed a plain metal pole for the observers of Festivus. The only decorations Clara hadn't been able to figure out yet were the—

"Pentacles?" she asked Grant, who had affixed himself to her side since concluding his rounds of guest-mongering. He was lifting for a sip from the tumbler of bourbon he'd been nursing all night before lowering it again to look at Clara with confusion.

"What pentacles?" he asked.

She gestured toward the display on the other side of the room near the rest of the holiday icons.

"Oh, those pentacles," he said. "For Solstice. The incense, too. Don't want to leave out the Wiccans."

"I wondered what that was I smelled."

"Mostly frankincense and myrrh, I think," he said.

"Which brings it all full circle," Clara replied with a smile.

She was about to say something more about how there really were a lot of December holidays when Hank ran up, clutching a misshapen paper star that was painted bright purple, sprinkled with neon pink glitter and tied with a chartreuse ribbon. He thrust it up toward her.

"Mama, look! Another ordament for our Christmas tree!"

"Or-*na*-ment," Clara corrected him automatically as she took the star from him, knowing she'd probably be correcting him another dozen times before Christmas actually arrived. "And it's beautiful, sweetie. I like the colors you picked."

"The or-*na*-ment lady helping us said we could pick whatever colors we want. I made another one that's orange and blue, but it's still drying."

Clara held up the ornament for Grant to see. "Now every year when we hang this on the tree, I'll think back on this moment and remember I was standing here with you when we got it."

It was true. Every year, when she or Hank hung it on the tree, she would be thinking fondly about the time she had spent with Grant this year, even if nothing ever came of it. She also knew she would be thinking about how she wished something *had* come of it, something that went beyond fondness, because that way, she would have another memory to carry with her.

Hank fairly beamed. "I made the other one for Grammy. Now she can think about me every year when she hangs it on her tree."

Without awaiting a reply, he spun around and ran back toward the room where the party organizers had set up the children's crafts. Which was just as well, since Clara had no idea how to tell him that his grandmother hired out their tree decorating, so she wasn't sure his star would even make it onto the Dunbarton tree. Though maybe now that Francesca had an original work of art from her grandson, she'd go back to doing their trimming the old-fashioned way.

"I guarantee you that Hank's star will be on our

tree every year," Grant said, clearly knowing what she was thinking. "And it will probably hang somewhere in Mom's office or bedroom the rest of the time."

Clara smiled. "Thanks. I kind of figured that, but it's nice to hear reassurance." She looked at the star again, then at the tiny cocktail purse she'd brought with her. "Now if I could just figure out what to do with it till we go home, so it doesn't get wrinkled. Well, any more wrinkled," she amended with a sigh.

"Here, let me have it," Grant said.

He took it from her hand and draped the loop of ribbon around his boutonniere, so that the garishly painted paper star—larger than his hand—dangled on his chest against his expensive suit for all the world to see. And if Clara hadn't already been halfway in lo— Uh, if Clara hadn't already been halfway enamored of him, that gesture would have finally put her there.

"There," he said. "That should keep it safe for the rest of the evening."

Yes, it should, she thought. Now if only Grant would do the same thing for her heart.

Nine

It was nearly midnight by the time the partygoers left for home. Hank was sacked before the car pulled away from the curb, so when they arrived back at the penthouse, Clara handed him over to Grant to carry upstairs. Hank murmured sleepily at the transfer, then looped his arms around his uncle's neck, nestled against his shoulder and fell asleep again. Clara tried not to notice how easily Hank curled into Grant or marvel at how much trust he had placed in him in such a short time. Instead, she battled another wave of affection for the man who had won that trust and showed such tenderness for her son.

Grant carried him effortlessly up to the penthouse and, after Francesca murmured her good-night to her grandson and gave him a kiss on the cheek, continued the journey back to Hank's…or rather, his father's—why did Clara keep making that mistake?—old bedroom and laid him carefully on the bed. Then she removed Hank's shoes and the little clip-on necktie decorated with snowmen that his grandmother had bought for him—she'd also bought his little man suit that was a miniature version of Grant's—and tucked him in. It was no problem to let him sleep in his clothes. Hank wouldn't be wearing them again before they went home. Tomorrow, she thought further. No, today, she realized when she noted the time on the little rocket ship clock sitting on the nightstand. Which had arrived much too quickly.

In fact, she might as well just leave Hank's new outfit here, since she couldn't see him having an opportunity on Tybee Island to dress like a tiny businessman—unless it was for Halloween. But she could see Francesca finding lots of reasons for Hank to dress like his uncle here in New York.

Clara swallowed against a lump in her throat, brushed back his dark curls and pressed a light kiss to his forehead. She whispered, "Good night, Peanut," which was the nickname she'd given him when he appeared on her first ultrasound looking like one, but which she hadn't used since she'd decided on a name for him, before he was even born. Then she turned toward the bedroom door to leave.

She was surprised to see Grant leaning in the doorway, waiting for her, but was happy that he had stayed. As exhausted as she was from the evening and the hectic week before it, she was entirely too wound up to sleep. Or maybe it was something else that had put her in that state. Some churning eddy of emotions that wouldn't stay still long enough for her to identify any of them, but which were pounding against her brain and heart with the ferocity of a tsunami.

"Nightcap?" Grant asked when she was within whispering distance.

"Oh, yes. Please."

She followed him to the library and waited while he fixed their drinks. He poured a bourbon for himself, then reached into the wine rack for what was sure to be another very nice red for her. But Clara halted him. A very nice red wasn't going to cut it for her tonight.

"I'll have what you're having," she told him when the bottle was barely halfway out of its slot.

He looked surprised, but tucked the wine back into its resting place and tugged free the cork from the bourbon again instead. She watched as he splashed a few swallows of the amber liquor into a cut crystal tumbler like his—at home, Clara would have poured a drink like that into a juice glass decorated with daisies whose paint was beginning to fleck—and looked at her for approval. She shook her head.

"I'll have what you're having," she repeated. "Same generous two-and-a-half fingers."

"Okay," he said, pouring in a bit more. "Funny, but I didn't take you for a bourbon drinker."

"Normally, I'm not," she said. "But nothing in my life has been normal since August Fiver showed up at the bakery."

And nothing in her life would ever be normal again. That, really, was the reason Clara needed something a little more bracing tonight. She didn't know if it had been seeing Hank dressed like a little millionaire, or how out of place she'd felt in Dunbarton Industries' offices, or how out of place she still felt here in the penthouse, or a combination of all of those things and a million more to boot. But tonight, more than ever before, Clara felt the need for something to dull a reality that was too fast closing in. Her son had become part of a world that wasn't her own, and he would be spending much of his future living a life that had nothing in common with hers. And it would be that way forever.

When Grant turned around holding both their drinks, looking as much a resident of this alien world as her son was now, Clara realized he was part of the problem, too. Because over the past week, especially the past few days, it had become clear that Grant didn't belong in this world, either. Not really. He may have been born to it, and he may be reasonably comfortable in it, but he wasn't truly, genuinely happy here. As a child, he'd had much different plans for himself, and passions that had nothing to do with the existence he was plodding through now. He was living his life out of obligation, not because it was the one he had chosen for himself. With each new day, that had become more clear.

But what was also clear was that he had no intention of leaving it.

Clara thought back to the way he'd been when he answered the front door upon her and Hank's arrival. Had that been only seven days ago? It felt like a lifetime had passed since she had stepped over the Dunbarton threshold. Grant's reception that day had been formal and awkward, and he'd seemed to have no idea how to react to Clara *or* Hank. Since then, he'd taught her about aquarium fish, had made jokes about Plu-toad and had lain on the floor, gazing up at the stars with her. And tonight, he'd hung a gaudy child's creation from his lapel as if it were the Congressional Medal of Honor. That first day, he hadn't seemed capable of laughter or whimsy. That first day, he hadn't seemed capable of happiness. But tonight…

She looked at the star, still dangling from his lapel,

then at the careless smile on his face. Tonight, he seemed very happy indeed. And Clara would bet everything she had in the world that it wasn't because the office holiday party had gone off without a hitch. It was because, at some point over the past few days, Grant had gotten in touch with something in himself that had reminded him what his life could have been like if he hadn't turned his back on his childhood to dive headfirst into adulthood decades before he should have. Maybe it was having Hank around that had done that. Or maybe it was something else. Clara just hoped Grant kept in touch with that part of himself after she and Hank were gone.

They made their way into the living room in time to see Francesca in front of the Christmas tree, admiring the star from Hank that she had hung on it front and center. She turned when she heard them approach, and she was smiling, too.

"You know," she said, "maybe next year we should put up the tree and decorate the house ourselves instead of hiring the service."

"I think that's an excellent idea," Grant told her.

He unlooped the star from his boutonniere and placed it beside the one Francesca had hung. "Just for now," he told Clara. "You can take it home with you tomorrow. But they do look good there together."

"Yes, they do," Clara had to admit. She was going to hate breaking the two of them up.

Francesca looked at Clara. "Maybe you and Hank could come for Thanksgiving next year," she said. "And we could all decorate the day after. That's when the service usually comes."

Clara started to decline, since it had been tough enough to swing a trip during the holidays this year. But the hopeful look on Francesca's face made her hesitate. The bakery was closed on Thanksgiving—and on Mondays, too, for that matter—and it wasn't especially busy the day after, since most people had so many leftovers and were out raiding the shopping malls. She could maybe close that weekend, too, without taking too big a financial hit. Things didn't really start hopping until a few weeks before Christmas. Her employees would probably like having the extra time off after Thanksgiving, too. It might be possible.

"Let me crunch some numbers," she told Francesca. "And look at the calendar for next year. I'll see what I can do."

Francesca smiled. "It would be lovely to have you both here. Grant and I usually go out for Thanksgiving dinner, since Mrs. Bentley has the day off. But we could have her prepare something the day before and put it all in the fridge. Then we'd just have to heat it up."

Clara shook her head. "I'll do the cooking on Thanksgiving." Hastily, she amended, "I mean, I *would* do the cooking on Thanksgiving. If we're able to come. Which I'll see if we can."

Francesca looked both delighted and a little appalled. "But that's so much to do! And you don't want to have to work on a holiday."

"It wouldn't be work for me," Clara said, knowing that was true. "I enjoy it. I always cook for Hank and me and some of our friends who spend Thanksgiving with us."

Funny, but she suspected that, as much fun as it was to cook for friends, she'd enjoy it even more cooking for family. Even if the Dunbartons weren't, technically, her family. They were Hank's family. So, in a way, that made them her family, too. Extended family. But still family. Kind of. In a way. More than anyone else had ever been family to her.

Francesca smiled again. "That really would be lovely," she said.

She told them both good-night and cautioned them not to stay up too late, because she had plans for Clara and Hank tomorrow before they headed to the airport in the late afternoon. Clara waited for the internal cringing that usually came with the prospect of enduring more of Francesca's gadabout tourism, but it never materialized. Interesting. Or maybe not. In spite of not belonging here in the Dunbarton world, Clara was beginning to kind of like it. New York had turned out to be not such a scary place, after all. And Central Park, right across the street, was as lush and bucolic as anything she'd ever found in Georgia. Hank could still climb trees here, even if he couldn't pick fresh peaches from them. And he could still go barefoot from time to time. And who knew? Maybe there were even fireflies in the summer that he could catch in a jar.

As she and Grant moved to sit on the sofa, he loosened his tie and unbuttoned the top two buttons of his shirt, then shrugged off his jacket and tossed it over the arm. Clara toed off first one high heel, then the other, immediately after sitting down. It was then that she noticed the additional gifts under the tree. The last time she'd been in here, there had been only the four she and Hank secretly placed there. Now there seemed to be dozens.

"Wow. Francesca's been busy," she said.

Then she noted that the tag on the gift nearest her was addressed to Hank from "Uncle Grant."

"She even did some shopping for you," she added.

Grant looked mildly offended. "Hey, I'll have you know I did my own shopping."

Clara was even more surprised. He hadn't asked her for suggestions as to what Hank would like. That first day, he hadn't even seemed to know how to talk to a three-year-old. Now he was Christmas shopping for one? He really had come a long way over the past week.

"I'm sure he'll love whatever you got him," she said.

"Yes, he will," Grant replied with complete confidence.

"It was nice of you to think of him," Clara said. Then she looked at the pile of gifts again. "It was nice of Francesca, too."

She didn't add that Francesca shouldn't have overdone it the way she had. Somehow Clara knew Hank's grandmother would always overdo it where he was concerned. Funny, though, how that didn't bother her quite as much as it would have a week ago.

"Hank won't know what to think when he sees that all those gifts are for him," Clara said.

"Well, not *all* of them are for him," Grant told her.

Right. There were the ones from Hank and Clara to Grant and Francesca under there, too. Somewhere.

"I just hope you and Francesca like yours from us as much as I'm sure Hank will like his from y'all."

Grant said nothing in response to that, only gazed at her looking… Hmm. Actually, he was looking kind of smug. Happily smug. Maybe he'd had more to drink at the party than she'd thought.

Clara lifted her own drink to her lips and sipped carefully, letting the bourbon warm her mouth before swallowing, relishing the heat of the liquor as it passed through her throat and into her stomach, spreading warmth throughout her chest. "Oh, yeah," she murmured. “That’s what I needed. It has been such a—” She stopped before saying that it had been such a long week. Because, suddenly, the week hadn’t seemed long at all. She and Hank really were leaving much too soon. Finally, she finished, “Such a busy week.”

“I guess you’ll be happy to get back home,” Grant said softly. “Back to your routine.”

Clara wanted to agree with him. And she did agree with him. To a point. Yes, she would be happy to get back to Tybee Island. She’d be happy for her and Hank’s lives to go back to normal. She’d be glad to get back to work at the bakery. She’d even be glad to return to their tiny apartment. Regardless of where or what it was, there really was no place like home.

She should have been glad to be leaving New York. But she actually kind of liked New York. Even more, she kind of liked what New York had to offer. The parks and museums and fun stuff, sure. And the lions at the library and the pear blinis at the Russian Tea Room. But more than any of those, Clara liked the Dunbartons. Especially Grant Dunbarton. And even having only been here for a short time, it was going to be strange returning to the place where she had lived her entire life. Because now she had experienced life away from home. And strangely, life away from home, as weird and foreign as it was, was starting to feel a little like, well, home.

“Yes, it’ll be nice to get back to Tybee Island,” she said. “But it’ll also be…”

“What?” he asked when she didn’t finish.

She sighed. “I don’t know,” she said honestly. “It kind of feels like we’ll be returning to a different place from the one we left.”

She was about to say more—though, honestly, she

still wasn't sure what she was thinking or feeling at the moment—when something over Grant's shoulder caught her eye. Beyond the windows, fat, frilly flakes of white were tumbling from the night sky.

"Oh, look, Grant! It's snowing!"

She set her drink on the end table and rose from the sofa, crossing to the window as if drawn there by a magic spell. Snow was magic. At least, in her part of Georgia it was. As rare a sighting as Santa Claus himself. The flurry of white seemed to pick up speed as she gazed through the glass, blowing first left, then right, then spinning in circles. Beyond the snow, the lights of New York sparkled merrily, making the scene even more entrancing.

She sensed more than saw Grant move alongside her at the window, but she couldn't quite tear her gaze away from the falling snow. Or maybe there was another reason she didn't want to do that, a fear that if she looked at him in that moment, she might very well succumb to the enchantment of the snow, of New York, of the Dunbarton world and of Grant himself. And Clara couldn't afford to be enchanted. Not by any of it. Because enchantments were only as good as their magic. And as bewitching as it was, at some point, magic always failed.

"It doesn't snow down in Georgia?" he asked softly.

She shook her head. And focused on the snow. Because it kept her from focusing on the soft velvet of his voice that was as magical as everything else.

"Not where I've lived," she told him, keeping her voice quiet, too. "Not much, anyway. For sure, it never did like this. I kind of hoped it would snow while we were here—for Hank, I mean," she quickly amended, even though it was only a half-truth, "but the weather was so mild when we got here, and then I didn't check again to see if it was going to stay that way or get colder." Not that it seemed to have gotten colder. On the contrary, it was getting warmer all the time…

But then, Clara hadn't checked a lot of things this week, she realized now. Not the weather, not the time, not—

She looked at Grant again. Not her heart. And now it seemed as if it might be too late for all those things. Unless…

Not sure why she did it, just knowing she had to, Clara cupped her hand over his cheek, pushed herself up on tiptoe and pressed her mouth to his. She had thought he would be surprised by the kiss. She certainly was, and she was the one who instigated it. But he returned it as swiftly and intimately as if it was something the two of them did all the time. Then he wrapped his arms around her waist and pulled her against him, seizing control of the embrace completely. And for the first time in her entire life, Clara knew what it was to feel as if she was home. Really home. In the place she belonged more than anywhere else in the world. Grant kissed her as if she were a part of him, a part he'd lost a long time ago and only just regained. He kissed her as if she was as essential to life as the air he breathed. He kissed her as if he couldn't not kiss her. So she looped her arms around his neck and kissed him deeper still.

She didn't know how long they stood there embracing in front of the window—maybe seconds, maybe centuries. She only knew she never wanted to move away from him again. He kissed her mouth, her temple, her cheek, her jaw, her neck. And when Clara tilted her head back to give him better access, he drew his mouth lower, along her bare shoulder and back again, over her collarbone and down her breastbone, skimming his lips over the top of one breast where it was revealed by her dress and then the other. She tangled her fingers in his hair and relished the feel of his warm breath against her sensitive flesh. Then she gasped when he cupped a hand over her breast.

He turned to move them out of the window, pressing her against the wall as he pushed his body into hers and kissed her more deeply still, covering her breast again, scrambling her thoughts and heating every part of her. When he raked his thumb over her nipple through the fabric, she tore her mouth from his and cried out. So he buried his head in the curve where her neck joined her shoulder and dragged open-mouthed kisses over both. Clara was so lost in sensation that she barely noticed when he dropped a hand to the hem of her dress. But when he tugged it up over her thigh, then her hip, and bunched it at her waist, she gripped the back of his shirt in both fists, holding on for dear life. Her legs nearly buckled beneath her, though, when he cupped a hand on her fanny over the lace of her panties.

"Oh, God, stop," she gasped. "Grant, we have to stop."

He lifted his head to look at her, and for a moment, it was as if he'd never seen her before and couldn't imagine how they had become so passionately entwined. Then realization must have come crashing down on him. Hastily, he removed his hand from her bottom and pulled her dress back down over her legs. But he didn't move away from her.

"Right," he whispered. His breathing was ragged and labored. "I guess it's not a good idea."

Clara smiled at that. "Oh, it's a very good idea," she assured him.

At least, it was right now. And *right now* was all she

wanted to think about. Because it was the only thing she could be absolutely sure of. And right now, she wanted Grant absolutely.

His gaze locked with hers. "You're sure?"

"Yes," she said. "This just isn't a good place for it. Let's go to your room." When he still didn't move, and only continued to study her face as if he couldn't quite believe she was real, she added softly, "Now, Grant. I want you now."

He nodded, then, with clear reluctance, pushed himself away from her. He took her hand in his and led her out of the living room and down the hall to the spiral staircase that led to the bedrooms below. Clara had no idea how she was able to make it without stumbling, so shaky was her entire body, but finally, finally, they made it to his bedroom. It was dark, save the soft blue light of the aquarium that threw wavy white lines on the wall behind it, giving the place an otherworldly aura that was strangely fitting. Clara felt as if she was in another world at the moment. One she never wanted to leave.

He closed the door behind them—locking it, she noted gratefully, clearly thinking about Hank sleeping so close by—then turned to her again. Before she could say a word, he pulled her back into his arms and kissed her, taking up exactly where they left off. Except this time, when he moved his head down to trail soft, butterfly kisses along her neck and shoulder, he tucked his fingers into the top of her dress and nudged it down to bare her breasts. As he covered one with a big hand, he dropped his other hand to her hem again, drawing the garment up over her thighs and hips once more. Blindly, Clara jerked his shirttail from his trousers and freed the buttons one by one, pushing it open so she could rake her fingertips over the warm skin beneath.

Grant Dunbarton may have been a workaholic, she thought as she touched him, but he clearly worked out, too. She traced the elegant cant of his biceps and triceps, then ran her fingers along the bumps of muscle on his shoulders, chest and torso until she reached the buckle of his belt. Instead of unfastening it, though, she drove her hand lower, over the swell of his erection beneath his trousers. He was already hard and ready for her. She need only unfasten his fly to enjoy him flesh on flesh. But she waited on that, pressing her hand against him to palm him through his clothing, marveling at how he grew harder still.

He pulled his mouth from hers and sucked in his breath at her caress, but didn't stop her. He only stroked her breast with sure fingers, thumbing the nipple and tracing the curve. Every time Clara moved her hand on him, he drew his thumb over her, until they were both panting with desire. Finally—quickly—she unbuckled and unzipped him, dipping her hand into his trousers and through the opening in his boxers to wrap her fingers around him. He was…oh. So hard. So stiff. So big. She drove her hand down the solid length of him, then pulled it back up again, loving the way his entire body reacted to the stroke. So she did it again. And again. And again.

Until he wrapped his fingers tight around her wrist and halted her motions. Until he told her, "Your turn."

Before she could object, he cupped his hands over both her shoulders and spun her around so she was facing away from him. Then he gripped the top of her zipper and lowered it until he could push her dress down over her hips and legs to puddle around her ankles. Her bra went just as quickly—a simple flick of his fingers did it—then he pulled her against him, back to chest, and looped an arm around her waist to anchor her there. Good thing, too, since the heavy weight of him pressing into her fanny through her underwear made her legs go weak.

He dipped his head to her neck again, skimming his lips lightly along her shoulder, then moved his free hand back to her breast. For long moments, he only held her close and caressed her, then he moved his hand lower…and lower…and lower still, easing his fingers into the juncture of her thighs. Then he was touching her there, through her panties, fingering the damp fabric and folds of flesh beneath, pushing and pulling to create a delicious friction she never wanted to end. As she grew wetter, he ducked his hand under the lacy garment and rubbed her more insistently, until his fingers were sliding against her and in and out of her with an easy rhythm. Clara matched it with her hips, pushing back against him when he entered her and levering forward when he withdrew, her bottom rubbing his erection with every motion.

As they moved that way, his breathing became as ragged as hers. Then he was pulling her panties down along with his trousers, rolling on a condom and sliding himself between her legs. Finally, he pushed himself into her as easily as he had done with his fingers. Only this time, he filled her deeply. She sighed at the sensation of him inside her. So full. So thorough. So complete. She had forgotten how good it felt to be joined to another human being in the most intimate way possible. Oh…so good. She picked up the rhythm, once more, taking all of him. He opened his hand over her back, splaying his fingers wide, and pushed her forward, bending her at the waist so he could enter her more deeply still. All Clara could do was go along for the ride.

He pumped her that way for long moments. Then, just when she thought they would both go over the edge, he slowly—and with clear reluctance—withdrew. They shed what little clothing remained and made their way silently to the bed. He shoved back enough covers to make room for them, then sat on the side of the bed and pulled Clara toward him. When she was sitting in his lap, straddling him, he pulled her breast to his mouth and tongued its sensitive peak. Then he moved to the other. Then back to the first, sucking her deep into his mouth and raking her with his teeth. As he did, he traced the delicate line bisecting her bottom, up, then down, then up again.

Just when she thought she would explode with wanting him, he pulled his mouth away from her breast to look at her face. She threaded her fingers through his hair and gazed into those blue, blue eyes, nearly drowning. She wanted desperately to say something. Something he needed to know. Something she needed to tell him. But she couldn't find a single word to tell him how she felt. So she kissed him, long and hard and deep, and hoped it would be enough.

He cupped her face in his palms and kissed her back, with a gentleness and tenderness that was at odds with their steamy passion and the carnality of their position. Sex had never been like this for Clara, a balance of hot and sweet, of need and generosity, of take and give. It had always been too much of those first things and too little of those last. Until now. And now…

Grant moved his hand between her legs and began the sweet torture of his fingers again. Oh, *now*. She never wanted to leave this bed. This room. This place. She never wanted to be with another man again.

Just as that thought formed, he lifted her up and over his heavy length again, entering her more deeply than ever. As he curved his palms gently over her bottom, she twined her fingers possessively around his nape and her legs around his waist. Their bodies merged as one a second time, each complementing the other perfectly, each completing the other irrevocably. He was hers. She was his. At least, for now.

In one last, fluid motion, Grant turned their bodies so that Clara was lying beneath him. He braced his elbows on the bed by each of her shoulders and dropped his thumbs to her jaw. Then, as he caressed her face and gazed into her eyes, he buried himself as deeply in her as he could go. She wrapped her legs around his waist again and lifted her hips to meet him, sliding her hands down his slick back to hold him there. Over and over, he thrust into her. Over and over, she opened to him. Then, as one, they came, each crying out in their climax before slowly descending again.

Grant rolled his body to lie on his side next to her. He smiled as he looped a damp curl around his finger, and kissed her one more time. Sweetly this time. Chastely. As if the whole world hadn't just shattered beneath them.

And it occurred to Clara in that moment that *right now* with Grant would never be enough.

Ten

Grant awoke the way he did every morning—alone in his bed during the dark hours just before dawn, to the beeping of his alarm clock. No, wait—that wasn't actually true. Yes, he was alone in his bed, and yes, it was still dark, and yes, he had to slap his hand down on the alarm to shut it off. But usually he woke up rested and clearheaded and ready to rise from bed, then immediately launched into a mental rehearsal of all the things he had to do once he arrived at work. Today, he was anything but rested and clearheaded, and the last thing he wanted to think about was work. The first thing he wanted to do was make love to Clara again. Then he wanted to spend the rest of the day thinking about her. And work? No way. He'd much rather spend the day with Clara. Doing whatever they felt like doing. Even if that was nothing at all. And then he wanted to go to bed with her at day's end and make love with her again. Then he wanted to do the same thing the next day. And then the one after that. For weeks and months and years on end.

Oh, this wasn't good. Grant needed to wake up the way he always did. Because that was the way he lived his life. Every day. All day. Day in. Day out. One day at a time. If he ever strayed from his routine…

Well. He just might not make it through the day.

He rolled onto his side and stared at his aquarium, its pale blue night-light a soft counterpoint to the tumble of thoughts bouncing around in his brain. Normally, the sight of his fish gliding about in blissful ignorance of the world and its constant pressures made Grant feel calm. Normally, watching the slow parade of myriad colors and elegant motion put him in touch with a part of himself where lived all the merriment, fancy and simplicity he'd stowed away decades ago and never allowed to roam free. Normally, that was enough to keep him going for another day. But this morning, watching the dappled, indolent to-and-fro, he knew that a momentary reconnection with what he'd left behind wouldn't be enough. Because he'd awoken alone. And in the dark. And where those two things had never bothered him before, this morning, they bothered him a lot.

He rolled over again, to the other side of his bed, where Clara had slept for an hour or so, before waking up and telling Grant she needed to finish the night in her own bed. Before Hank awoke and went looking for her, she'd said. Before his mother awoke and saw the door to the guest bedroom open and the bed still made. Clara had kissed him one last time on the mouth, and smiled in a way that could have meant anything. Then she'd slipped back into her dress and stolen away like a thief in the night. Which was appropriate. She was a thief. She'd stolen something from Grant he might never get back. Especially if she took it with her when she returned to Georgia.

He lay his head on the pillow where hers had been only hours ago and inhaled deeply. Yeah, there it was. The faintest hint of cinnamon. The merest suggestion of ginger. And something else, too, something that was inherently Clara Easton. Something that could never be bottled the way spices were and opened whenever he wanted to enjoy it. Something he would never find anywhere else, no matter how hard he tried. And now she was going home, and she would be taking that with her, too.

He looked at the clock on the nightstand. 6:17 a.m. Seventeen minutes later than he always got up. Usually, by now, he was in the shower, readying himself for another day of running the family business that he'd never really wanted to run, but which had to be run by someone in the family because…

Because. He was sure there was a reason for that. He was sure there had been one when he shouldered the responsibility so many years ago. But he couldn't quite remember now what that reason was. There was one, though. There must be. He was sure of it.

He couldn't take the day off, as much as he might want to. Even being the boss had its limits. Grant had a meeting this morning that had been on his agenda for weeks, a meeting that had been nearly impossible to organize in the first place, thanks to the schedules of everyone involved. He couldn't miss it. He was the one who had called for it. Clara's plane didn't leave until this evening. He could head home after the meeting and be back in time to take her to the airport himself. It shouldn't go past noon. One at the latest. Two at the outside. Even that would give him a two-hour window to get her and Hank to LaGuardia. But he wouldn't make the meeting at all if he didn't get a move on and get into the shower now.

He rose and shrugged on his robe, then headed for the bedroom door to make the short trip up the hall to the bathroom. Instead of heading left, however, he turned right. He strode past the closed door to Hank's room and paused at the one opposite. He started to knock quietly, then figured he probably shouldn't wake Clara. Just because he wanted to see her before he went to work. Just because he was having trouble thinking about anything but her. Just because it would be nice to have a smile from her to carry with him for the rest of the day.

He should leave her a note, he thought. To tell her he would be home in time to take her to the airport for her flight. No, to tell her how much he'd enjoyed last night, and that he would be home in time to take her to the airport for her flight. There was just one problem. How could he possibly convey how much he'd enjoyed last night in a note?

He'd call her before the meeting. There would be just enough time after he got to work. It would be good to hear her voice, anyway. It had been hours since he'd heard her voice. Eons. Just hearing her say "Good morning" would be enough to get him through the day. At least until he saw her again this afternoon.

For a moment, Grant only stood with his open palm against the bedroom door. He really wished he didn't have to go to work today. He couldn't remember a time when he'd ever felt that way. But he did today. Then he reminded himself that the sooner he got to work, the sooner he could call Clara. So, morning planned, he headed down the hallway again.

So he wasn't going to call or anything.

Clara looked at the pile of bags by the Dunbartons' front door—the two she and Hank had arrived with and two additional, newer and bigger ones for him, thanks to his and Francesca's negotiations about what he would be taking back to Georgia with him right away because he just couldn't live another minute without it. Would that Clara was able to do the same. But Grant probably would have objected to being packed up in such a way. Then she looked at Hank, who was giving his grandmother one final hug before they left. Then she looked at Renny Twigg, who had arranged for a car from Tarrant, Fiver & Twigg to take Clara and Hank to the airport, the way Gus Fiver had arranged for one to pick them up there…had it only been a week ago? Funny, Clara felt as if it had been a lifetime since she and Hank showed up at the Dunbartons' front door like a couple of secondhand relations.

"We should get going," Renny said gently. "Traffic and all."

Clara nodded. "Hank, sweetie," she said, "it's time to go."

Francesca had wanted to come to the airport with them, but Clara had told her it was okay, that if she did, it would be hours before she got back home, and that it would be easier for all of them if Renny had the driver just drop her and Hank off. A long goodbye wouldn't be good for any of them.

Of course, if Grant had been there—or if he had, oh, Clara didn't know…maybe offered to drive her and Hank to the airport himself, say—it would have been a different story. She would have taken the longest goodbye she could get from him. Evidently, though, he wasn't going to give her a goodbye at all. He'd already left for work by the time she woke up, and she hadn't heard a word from him all day. No text. No call. No email he could have fired off from his desk. She hadn't expected sonnets from him. Or even a haiku. But she would have liked to hear *some*thing. A few words or emojis to let her know he was thinking about her and that last night had meant more to him than…

What? she asked herself. The way she was thinking, it almost seemed as if it had meant something more to her than…well, whatever it had meant. A physical reaction to a sexual attraction they'd both been feeling all week. Her attempt to exorcise a bundle of turbulent emotions that had been bouncing around in her head and heart demanding release. An effort to make sense of something that defied sensibility. She still wasn't sure what last night had been, so how could she expect Grant to think it was more than any of those things? Still, it would have been nice if he had at least acknowledged that it happened, if he had let her know he'd thought about her once or twice today.

Because she sure hadn't been able to stop thinking about him.

She'd hated leaving his bed to return to her own last night. But she had been afraid Hank might wake up fretful, which he sometimes did after going to bed so late following a highly stimulating event like the party. And if he'd come looking for her in the guest room and seen she wasn't there, or that her bed hadn't been slept in…

Well, she just hadn't wanted to make him think she wasn't there for him when he needed her, that was all. And at the other end of the spectrum, if Francesca had seen that Clara never went to her own bed, she might have thought something was going on between her and Grant that would…

Well, she just hadn't wanted to make Francesca think there was a chance Clara was falling in love with her other son, thereby ensuring her grandson would be linked to her more decisively than before. Even if Clara was kind of falling in love with Francesca's other son.

That was obviously a pipe dream. Grant hadn't even waited around long enough to tell her good morning. How could she have expected him to be here to say goodbye?

"You've been wonderful, Francesca," Clara said as she and Hank finally ended their hug. "I can't thank you and Grant enough for making us feel so welcome here."

"But you *are* welcome here," Francesca told her, sounding vaguely alarmed that Clara might not think so. "Any time, under any circumstances. I'm already making plans for your next visit. Can you believe we never made it to a show?" she added, sounding scandalized. "How can anyone come to New York and not see a show? You must come back as soon as it's convenient."

Clara forced a smile. "We'd like that."

She looked down at her son, who had moved away from Francesca to affix himself to Clara's side the same way he had that first morning. Except this time, any apprehension he might be feeling was because he didn't want to leave. Neither did Clara. But there was no way she could take any more time from the bakery, and Hank needed to get back to his routine before he forgot what it was.

"Maybe you could come visit us on Tybee Island," she told Francesca. That way, there wouldn't be the risk of running into Grant. "Hank's preschool has spring break in April. Come down for Easter. I'll bake a giant ham and a sweet potato casserole, and we can have bacon-braised green beans and cheese grits for sides and banana pudding for dessert. How does that sound?"

"It sounds like my cholesterol will go through the roof," she said with a smile. "But I'd like that very much. Maybe I can convince Grant to take time away from work to come with me."

Clara started to object, then decided it wouldn't be necessary. There was little chance Grant would take time away from work for anything. So Clara said nothing at all.

"I'll miss you, Grammy," Hank said.

His eyes grew moist, but he swiped at them with one fist. It was all the encouragement Francesca needed. Her eyes went misty, too. Not that Clara could blame either of them. She felt like crying herself. Though maybe for a slightly different reason…

Hank broke away for one more hug, then Renny Twigg echoed their need to leave. At the same time, the doorbell rang, heralding the arrival of their driver and a doorman with a luggage cart to carry down the bags. Francesca promised again to pack up the gifts under the tree and ship them to Tybee Island tomorrow, though Hank had opened one this morning after she had insisted. Inside had been a plush, squishy planet Jupiter, complete with arms, legs and smiling face, that Hank hadn't put down since. He'd also kicked science to the curb by naming it Plu-toad.

The flurry of bag-gathering and final goodbyes dried whatever tears were left, and then Hank, Clara and Renny were in the elevator with the driver and doorman, heading down to the lobby. Clara surreptitiously checked her phone as they descended, to see if there were any new texts. There weren't. Then she checked to see if she'd missed a call. She hadn't. Email? Nope.

Then the elevator doors were opening, and she and Hank and Renny were following their driver and luggage toward the door. Once through it, Clara looked up and down Park Avenue. But there was no handsome, dark-haired, blue-eyed man in a power suit running toward them shouting, "Clara! Wait!" the way there would have been if this were the Hollywood version of the story. So once she and Renny were settled inside the car with Hank fastened into his car seat, there was no reason for her to look back.

This wasn't Hollywood, Clara reminded herself as the car pulled away from the curb. And, like Hollywood, it wasn't real life, either. The Dunbarton family lived in a way few people were able to manage, in a world few people ever entered. Hank may have been her ticket into it, but she would always be here temporarily, and always as a fringe dweller. She would never be a permanent resident, and she would never really belong. It was time she started accepting that and went back to the life she knew. The life to which she'd been born. The life where she belonged. The life she—usually—loved.

The life that would never be the same again.

Grant sat at the head of the giant table bisecting the boardroom of Dunbarton Industries, glaring at the man seated halfway down the left side. Not just because he was the reason this meeting had gone on hours too long—so long that Clara and Hank must, by now, be on their way to LaGuardia without him—but because he had spent the majority of those hours contributing to the very problems Grant had called this meeting to avoid. He hadn't even had a chance to slip out and call

Clara to tell her goodbye, because the meeting had become so contentious he hadn't wanted to risk making it worse by breaking for anything. He'd even arranged for lunch to be brought in, because by that point, he'd been worried everyone might leave and not come back.

It had been that way since the moment Grant arrived at work. He'd exited the elevator to hear voices raised in controversy and had entered the reception area to see that two members of the meeting had already arrived and were engaged in not-so-civil debate over the only item on the agenda—Dunbarton Industries' acquisition of an abandoned wharfside property in an area a group of historians had halfheartedly slated for revitalization once upon a time. But the Waterfront Historical Society had been forced to scrap the project when the economy tanked, and the massive warehouse complex had been sitting vacant and decaying for years. Grant wanted to buy and revamp all of it to make it a safe, environmentally friendly work and living space, the centerpiece of what could potentially become an industrial-retail-entertainment-residential complex. He'd invited a handful of the city's leading developers to attend today, knowing a number of them would be interested. All he should have had to do was iron out a few minor problems that might arise with Dunbarton Industries and some of the other involved parties, and they'd be set. He'd figured that part of the meeting would take, at most, a couple of hours. Then it would just come down to a matter of which developer could offer the most attractive package to all involved, which should have taken no time at all.

Unfortunately, the developer he had considered the best fit for the enterprise had, unbeknownst to him, already had a number of run-ins with the Waterfront

Historical Society that had either ended very badly or hadn't ended at all. Both sides had used the first part of the meeting to try to iron out those problems instead of the ones they were supposed to be talking about. It hadn't taken long for everything to escalate to the point where now *everyone* at the table was bickering about past wrongs. Every time Grant thought he had things back on track, someone—usually the man half-way down the table on the left side—drove everything over a cliff again. Try as he might to point out how well his proposal could benefit most of the people present, most of the people present preferred to talk about—or argue about—something else instead.

Sometimes Grant felt like the world of big business was populated by nothing but three-year-olds. No, wait. That wasn't true. Hank Easton was three, and he behaved better than anyone currently seated in the Dunbarton Industries boardroom. At this point, it was beginning to look as if Grant would never see Hank or his mother again.

Then again, whose fault was that? Grant was the boss here. He was the one who called the meeting. He could have also called an end to it any time he wanted today and then tried to reconvene at some point when everyone was more amenable to making progress. But he hadn't. Instead, he'd done everything he could to ensure it *didn't* end. At least not until he achieved the outcome from it he hoped—no, needed—to achieve. The acquisition of that property could ultimately be worth billions in company revenue. It could be the biggest success Dunbarton Industries ever had. They weren't the only company interested in it. Waiting even a week could mean another company swooped in and grabbed all that potential for itself. Grant needed to act quickly if he wanted this thing to succeed for them. And, hey, wasn't success the whole point to life? Wasn't that why he worked as hard as he did? So that the family business would thrive?

Yes, yes and yes. At least, all of that had been true before. Before Clara Easton and her son showed up at his front door.

He looked at the group of people surrounding the table again. There were eight of them. At least four of them besides him would be affected positively by this arrangement if he could pull it off. Those four represented dozens more who would become involved further down the road and benefit. From those dozens, hundreds more. In the long run, if this project worked out the way Grant envisioned it, it would create thousands of jobs, most of them permanent. A dangerous public eyesore would become a safe, walkable area with green space. Property values would rise. Investors would reap rewards. From a business standpoint, it could be a massive success.

From a business standpoint.

But what about other standpoints? What about other successes? Clara was on her way home to Georgia, and Grant hadn't even told her goodbye. And who knew when he would see her again? She had a business to run eight hundred miles away from the one he had to run here. They both had commitments to their work that were equally demanding. And hell, it wasn't as if they'd made any commitments beyond those. It wasn't as if they'd made a commitment to each other. On the contrary, Clara had told him last night she wanted him "now." Maybe that meant she wanted him in the heat of that moment. Maybe it meant she only wanted him that once. She had left his bed to return to her own afterward. Sure, she'd had a good reason for it. But she had left his bed to return to her own.

And he hadn't stopped her.

No commitment. From either of them. No promises. No plans. No talk of the future at all. But that was good, right? It meant neither of them had expected anything more from last night than one night. Yes, they would see each other again eventually. They would have to, since Hank was a part of the Dunbarton family now. But Clara…

Clara had offered no indication that she wanted to be part of the family, too. At least in any capacity beyond the one that included her son. She'd had to get back to Georgia for her work. She couldn't come visit New York over Hank's spring break because of her work. Grant couldn't visit her in Georgia for the same reason. Both of them had put their work first. Both had made that their priority.

He could still end this meeting now. If he hurried, he might even make it to LaGuardia before her plane left. If nothing else, he could call for a ten-minute break that would allow him to retreat to his office long enough to call Clara and tell her goodbye.

He glanced at his phone, sitting on the table to his right. It had gone off a number of times during the meeting, but always with notifications he knew he could attend to later. Not once had it gone off with a notification from Clara. She was leaving without telling him goodbye, too.

And maybe that, really, told Grant everything he needed to know. About himself and Clara both.

"All right," he said to the group seated around the table. "Let's start from the top. Again."

* * *

"Did you have a good time in New York?"

It took a moment for Clara to realize Renny Twigg was speaking to her. Hank had been chattering at the other woman ever since the car pulled away from the curb, recapping everything he'd done with his grandmother over the past week. And Renny, bless her heart, had hung on every word. Funny, but Clara wouldn't have pegged her as someone who would respond as well as she did to a toddler. Not that the high-powered lawyer life seemed especially fitting for her, either. Renny definitely gave off a vibe that made her seem as if she was more suited to a life away from suits. Clara had no idea why, but somehow, she pictured her being the kind of woman who would be happier in a job where she could corral livestock.

"I did," Clara said in response to her question. Because she had mostly had a good time in New York. The fact that her heart had been broken there at the end didn't change that.

"Was it your first time?" Renny asked.

Once again, it took a moment for Clara to reply. Because for a moment, she thought Renny was referring to something that really wasn't any of her business and frankly should have been obvious with Hank, the fruit of Clara's loins, sitting right there. Then she thought maybe Renny meant something else that still wasn't any of her business—jeez, Clara was just realizing herself that it was hard to recognize the first time you fell in love with someone. But of course, Renny was talking about coming to New York.

"Yes," she said. "It was my first time." In New York *and* in love.

"What did you think?" Renny asked.

"It's not what I expected at all," Clara told her. Not New York. And not love, either.

"It always surprises people," Renny said.

Well, Clara could certainly understand why.

"They expect it to be this huge, overwhelming thing where they'll never feel comfortable or safe."

Yep, that was pretty much the way Clara had always thought about love.

"They're scared they'll get robbed or end up so lost they'll never be able to find their way."

Exactly, Clara thought.

"But after a while, they realize it's not so scary. And it can be…*so* wonderful. And then people can't believe they waited so long."

Well, Clara didn't know about that. New York, sure. She agreed with everything Renny said. But love? Not so much. Because Clara had indeed been robbed while she was here—Grant had stolen her heart. And she was certain she'd never be able to find her way back to the place where she was before she came here. And she definitely didn't know if she'd ever feel comfortable or safe again. Not the way she'd felt comfortable and safe with Grant. So for now, the score was New York, one, Clara nil, and Grant…

Well, Grant had certainly scored, she couldn't help thinking. Unfortunately, it was looking as if, now that he had, he wanted to drop out of the game completely.

Gee, he had a lot more in common with his brother than she'd thought.

Their arrival at the Delta terminal of LaGuardia airport came way too quickly for Clara's comfort. So much for New York City's notorious rush hour traffic. Then again, when she glanced down at her watch, it was to see the trip had taken them more than forty-five minutes. She'd just been so lost in her thoughts, she hadn't even noticed the passage of time.

With any luck, it would continue to pass quickly once she and Hank were back on Tybee Island. She'd just have to make sure she threw herself into her work once they were home. Work was good for passing time and keeping her focused on the things she should be focusing on. And it was good for making her forget the things she should be forgetting about.

Things like the pale blue eyes of a man who refused to let himself be happy.

Eleven

Clara did her best to take a page from the Grant Dunbarton workaholic playbook when she got back to Tybee Island, throwing herself into the ebb and flow of the bakery to the point where she thought about nothing else—save Hank, of course. But now that Hank was inextricably tied to the Dunbartons, thinking about him—and talking to him and being with him—meant she would always be thinking about them, too. And thinking about them meant thinking about Grant, which then made her all the more determined to throw herself into her work and think about nothing else save Hank.

Which only started the cycle all over again.

It was exhausting, frankly, trying to focus on nothing but work, from the moment she rose in the morning until she switched off the light at night. She didn't see how Grant lived this way. No wonder he'd been so joyless.

No, she told herself. That wasn't right. He wasn't joyless. At least, he hadn't been at the end of her time in New York. But more than a week had passed since she and Hank had left, and Clara hadn't heard a word from Grant *or* Francesca, save a quick call to the latter immediately after their arrival back in Georgia to let her know they'd arrived home safely. Silence from Grant hadn't surprised her. Well, okay, it had. Part of her had thought he was starting to break away from the relentless CEO who had usurped his childhood and get back in touch with the little boy who'd wanted to head up a nonprofit called KOOK. But silence from Francesca? The mother of all grandmothers? That had surprised Clara a lot. She would have thought Francesca would be calling every day.

But it was Christmas, she reminded herself, and people got busy over the holidays. She knew that, because she felt as if she was single-handedly catering every holiday party on the island. Francesca was probably just so bogged down in entertaining and being entertained that she didn't have a minute to spare for anything else.

The timer on the big oven went off, pulling Clara's thoughts back to the matter at hand—snowman cookies. Two dozen of them. For starters. They were destined for the holiday party at Hank's preschool tomorrow—the last day of class before Christmas, which was scarcely a week away—along with dozens more. Clara had baked Christmas tree cookies, too, along with dreidel cookies and kinara cookies and New Year's baby cookies and pentacle cookies.

Well, who knew? She didn't want to leave out the Wiccans. Or maybe she'd just been thinking too much about the last night she'd spent in New York. And not just the party at Dunbarton Industries. About making love with Grant, too.

But she wasn't going to think about him, she reminded herself. Again. She was going to think about work. Unfortunately, going back to work meant looking at two dozen Rudolph cookies she'd frosted earlier that were set enough now to go into one of the cases in front. And seeing those just reminded Clara of Grant all over again, and how she'd told him the story of the Rudolph ornament in her former foster home that she'd nurtured and repaired and hadn't been allowed to take with her when she'd been reassigned. What had possessed her to tell him that story? She'd never told that story to anyone.

Stop. Thinking. About. Grant. She really did need to focus on work. Which, naturally, made her think of Grant. Gah.

Hastily, she picked up the tray with all the Rudolphs staring at her and carried them out to the shop. The bell over the door was ringing to announce yet another customer—gee, she hoped they could fit another customer in here, since the shop was already full to the gills—so Clara threaded her way through her three busy salesclerks, toward the cookie case, to tuck the tray into an empty spot. And wow, there were a lot of empty spots. At this point, she was going to be baking until midnight Christmas Eve if she wanted to have something for Hank to leave out for Santa.

She slid the Rudolphs into the case and was heading back to the kitchen to retrieve more cookie dough from the walk-in when Tilly cupped a hand over her shoulder to halt her.

"Is it too late for someone to place a special order?" she asked.

Well, it was, Clara thought. Christmas was only eight days away, and she'd taken on about as many special orders as she could manage for what was left of the holidays. But depending on what the customer wanted, she might be able to squeeze in one more.

"Maybe," she told Tilly. "What does she need?"

"It's not a she," Tilly said. "It's a he."

The comment immediately carried Clara back to the day Gus Fiver entered the bakery and turned her world upside down. She pushed the thought away. Her world would get back to normal, she told herself. Eventually. Someday. Okay, it would get back to a new kind of normal. She just had to figure out what it was going to be.

"All right, what does *he* need?" she asked Tilly.

Before the salesclerk could respond, a voice—much too deep to be Tilly's, but infinitely more familiar—replied loudly enough to be heard over the buzz of the customers, "You, Clara. He needs you."

The crowd went silent at the announcement, every head turning to see who had spoken. When Clara followed their gazes, she saw Grant on the other side of the counter, standing head and shoulders above and behind the group of women who had been waiting to be served. Though they now seemed much more interested in waiting to see what happened next. They parted like the Red Sea to reveal him from head to toe, then, as one, looked back at her, to see how she would respond.

"Uh, hi," was all she could manage.

The heads turned toward Grant.

When he realized they had an audience, he grinned. With absolute, unadulterated joy and genuine, unbridled playfulness. Which, Clara couldn't help thinking, wasn't exactly the reaction she might have expected from a joyless, relentless, workaholic CEO. He wasn't dressed like one, either. He wasn't even dressed like a CEO on vacation. No, Grant Dunbarton looked like any other island local, in knee-length surf jams, a Savannah Sand Gnats sweatshirt and Reef Rover shoes.

"Hi yourself," he greeted her in return.

If Clara didn't know better, she could almost believe it was Brent Dunbarton, not Grant, who had ambled into her bakery. Except for one noticeable difference. She'd never come close to being in love with Brent. But the man standing in her bakery now?

Well, there was a time when she had thought she might love him. Before he'd chosen his work over his own happiness. Before he'd chosen his work over her and her happiness, too.

The heads had turned again, to get Clara's reaction. But she wasn't as comfortable being the center of attention as Grant obviously was, so she tilted her head toward the door that connected the shop to the kitchen in a silent invitation for him to follow her. The disappointment of the crowd was palpable—a couple of women even *Aww*ed or muttered *C'mon, Clara*, but she didn't care. She was happy to provide them fodder for their holiday parties. Not so much to provide fodder for the coconut telegraph.

She trusted Grant to follow, because she wasn't about to turn around and look at all those speculative faces. The only speculation she was interested in the moment was her own. What was he doing here? Dressed the way he was? Why hadn't he called first? Or texted? Or, jeez, sent up a flare? He could have at least given her some small notice, so she wouldn't have to be greeting him in her once-white-now-rainbow-hued baker duds of formerly white pajama pants, T-shirt and head scarf. And—*Oh, no*, she thought when she saw her wavy reflection in the silver door of the walk-in—her now rainbow-hued face, too.

She grabbed a towel from the counter and did her best to scrub the remnants of frosting and chocolate from her face. Then she spun around to face Grant… who had somehow become even more handsome and sweet looking in the handful of seconds it had taken them to escape the crowd.

But she wouldn't succumb to a sweet and a handsome face. Especially one that couldn't even be bothered to call her. Still, he had come here for something. She couldn't imagine what, but the least she could do was hear him out.

"Okay, let's try this again," she said. "Hi."

He grinned again. "Hi yourself," he repeated.

An unwieldy silence ensued. Mostly because Clara had no idea what to say. Seriously, why was he here? And how could a man who had rejected her in favor of a corporate conglomerate still stir so many feelings inside her she didn't want to feel? She needed to get back to work. *Best wind this up ASAP.*

In spite of that, she asked lamely, "So… How's things?"

He chuckled. Honestly, she could just smack him for looking so—

Happy. Oh, God, he looked *happy*! How could he be so happy when he'd made her feel so lousy?

"Um, different," he said.

She gave his outfit an obvious once-over. "So I see."

He sobered a little at that. "Yeah, I guess I look a lot like Brent, don't I? I didn't mean to—"

"No," she interrupted him. "You don't. I could easily tell the two of you apart. You look nothing like Brent. You *are* nothing like Brent. But you know, for all his faults, at least your brother followed his heart and fulfilled his dreams and lived his life in a way that made him happy. But you… You'd rather…"

When she trailed off without finishing—mostly because she was afraid she wouldn't be able to do that without revealing just how hurt she was—he asked, "I'd rather what?"

She shook her head, still not trusting her voice or herself to answer.

He took a step closer. She took one in retreat. He frowned at her withdrawal.

"C'mon, Clara," he said softly. "I'd rather what?"

She inhaled a deep breath, crossed her arms over her midsection, arrowed down her brows and tried again. "You've buried your dreams, Grant. Your life is nothing but your work. It means more to you than anything—anyone—else ever will. And your heart? Jeez, there's a part of me that sometimes wonders if you really have one."

He winced at that last, closing his eyes and turning his head as if she really had smacked him. Then he opened his eyes and looked at her again, his gaze unflinching this time.

"Why didn't you call me to tell me goodbye before you left New York?" he asked.

It wasn't exactly what Clara had expected him to say. Nor was it a question she knew how to answer. So she only said, "What?"

He shrugged. "Why didn't you call me to tell me goodbye before you left New York?"

She studied him a moment longer before answering. Finally, truthfully, she said, "I don't know."

He was right. She could have called him to say goodbye. Or she could have texted him. Or sent him an email. She just…hadn't. She'd been too focused that day on getting herself and Hank packed and ready for their flight back to Georgia. Because she had needed to get Hank back into his routine here, and because she had needed to get herself back to...

Work. She hadn't been able to spend any more time in New York, because it had been too important for her to get back to the bakery, which would be incredibly busy before Christmas. There was no way she'd have any time for things like…

But she had a business to run, she reminded herself. And she had employees who depended on her for their weekly paycheck. It wasn't that she had chosen her work over Grant. It was that…

She sighed again. It was that she had chosen her work over Grant. Because her work was important. Because she had obligations. Because people were relying on her.

"Wow," she said softly. "I guess we're both a couple of workaholics, aren't we?"

He nodded slowly.

"And I guess we've both sort of lost sight of what's really important."

He took another step toward her. This time, Clara didn't take one in retreat. "So what are we going to do about that?" he asked.

She shook her head and replied honestly again. "I don't know."

He studied her again. But he didn't say anything.

So Clara did the only thing she could. She nodded toward his shirt and said, "I thought you were a fan of the Savannah Clumps of Kelp."

He expelled a single chuckle—it was a start. To what? She still wasn't sure. But something inside her that had been wound too tight gradually began to unknot. “What, those losers?” he asked. “Nah. The Sand Gnats are where it’s at.”

She braved a smile. “I’m glad you’ve seen the light.”

Now he sobered again. “Yeah, I have. And not just there. A whole lot of things have come clear to me in the last couple of weeks.” He took a step closer. “Thanks to you.”

Clara took a step closer, too. He was trying to meet her halfway. That was a little better than a start. The least she could do was help him get there. “Oh?” she asked.

He moved closer. “Yeah.”

She did likewise. “In what way?”

By now, they were nearly toe-to-toe and almost eye to eye thanks to Clara’s height in her work clogs. There was still an inch or two separating them—both distance-wise and stature-wise—but it wouldn’t take much work for either of them to close that distance. Should either of them want to. Grant seemed to be trying to do that. Clara wished she knew how to help him.

“I resigned from Dunbarton Industries,” he told her. “Effective immediately.”

Her mouth dropped open at that. She couldn’t help it. He might as well have just told her there was a giant squid dancing the merengue behind her, so astonishing and fantastic was the announcement.

But all she managed for a response was, “You did?”

He nodded. “I did. But it’s taken some time to get the kinks ironed out of the arrangement, and I didn’t want to say anything to anybody until we knew it would all work out the way we wanted it to.”

“We?” Clara asked.

He nodded again. “Mom and I. She’s taking over as CEO.” He smiled again. “Effective immediately.”

Clara’s mouth almost dropped open again. Almost.

But somehow that news wasn't quite as astonishing or fantastic as the other had been. She'd seen for herself how at home Francesca was at the Dunbarton Industries holiday party, and how much the employees liked her. And she'd seemed to really know what she was doing when she went over the budget. From what Clara had seen, Francesca had been passionate about her ideas for keeping the company running. She'd been one of its vice presidents once upon a time. And she was a Dunbarton. Why shouldn't she run the family business if she wanted to? As long as she wanted to.

"And Francesca is okay with that?" Clara asked. Even with all the other considerations, Francesca hadn't exactly been Ms. Corporate America while Clara and Hank were in New York. She'd been much more Ms. Grandmother America.

"Yeah, she is," Grant said. "The minute you and Hank left, she started feeling aimless. She wanted to call you two the day after you left but was afraid you'd think she was being intrusive and trying to insinuate herself into your life down here or trying to bribe Hank to tell you to bring him back to New York."

"I would never think that about Francesca," Clara protested.

When Grant raised a single brow in response, she relented. "Okay, maybe I thought that about Francesca at first," she admitted. "But that was just the leftover foster kid in me being insecure and fearful."

"Anyway," Grant continued, "When I told her I wanted to step down from the company—hell, not just step down, but leave it completely—she just kind of smiled and told me it was about time. She'd always known following in my father's footsteps hadn't made me happy, but that it had seemed so important to me, she didn't question it. She said she'd always known I would finally figure out what I really wanted and pursue that instead, and wondered what took me so long. She'd always planned to take over for me when that happened, and that was why she stayed on the board and kept a finger in what was going on in the business. Now she'll have something to keep herself occupied so she won't miss Hank as much." His grin returned as he added, "And, unlike *some* CEOs, she'll be the kind of boss to give herself time off for the things she really wants to do. Like be with her grandson when he comes to visit."

Clara grinned back. "So you finally figured out what you want?"

"Yeah," he said. "And I wonder what took me so long, too. Then I remembered what I want didn't come into my life until recently, so there was really no way I could know that. Not until…"

"Until?" Clara asked.

"Until I met you."

She smiled.

"And Hank, too," he added. "But mostly you. The day you left New York was just…" He blew out an exasperated breath. "Actually, the day at work was like every other day. Except that by the end of the day, I knew there was something besides work I could be doing. Something I *wanted* to be doing. A lot more than I wanted to be working, that's for damned sure. Before you, Clara, I could pretend my work gave my life purpose, that it was important …" He made that exasperated sound again. "Before you, I could pretend I was happy," he finally said. "Or, at least, happy enough."

"'Happy enough' doesn't sound like happy," Clara told him.

"It's not. I know that now. I could never go back to

being the workaholic CEO after that night you and I..." He halted, and there was something in his eyes that made her heart turn over. "I couldn't be that again after that night, Clara. Hell, I could barely maintain that veneer the whole time you were in New York. The minute you stepped through the door, you started reminding me of too many things I'd made myself forget. Things that made me happy when I was a kid. Things that made me want to be happy as an adult. But I felt like I could only go after those things if I turned my back on what I thought was my duty to my family. I'd completely forgotten about my duty to myself."

Wow, did that sound familiar. Not the part about being reminded of a happy childhood, since Clara's hadn't exactly been that. But the part about wanting to be happy as an adult. She, too, had convinced herself she was "happy enough." She had Hank and a reasonably solid business, and she kept a roof over both. But she'd been pretty driven to ensure things stayed that way. She put nearly every hour of her day into something else—being a mom or being a businesswoman, thinking she could only do those things by not thinking about herself. When was the last time she had been just Clara? Really, had she *ever* been just Clara?

"So what will it take to make you happy as an adult?" she asked him.

"I think you already know that," he said.

"I'd still like to hear you say—"

"You," he told her without hesitation.

"—it."

Wow, this was going to work out so well. Because the only other thing she needed to be happy—happy for just Clara—was Grant.

She took a final step forward that literally brought

her toe-to-toe with him. And then she tipped herself up on her toes and pressed her mouth to his. It was a glorious kiss, even better than the first one they'd shared. Because this time, there was no doubt. This time, there was only...

Joy. Complete, unmitigated, take-no-prisoners joy. And if there was one thing the world needed more of at Christmas—and one thing Clara and Grant needed more of forever—it was joy. Lucky for both of them, it could be found just about anywhere. All you had to do was look for it. Or, if you were very lucky, joy came looking for you. Clara was just glad it had found her and Grant both.

It was snowing in New York City, Clara saw as she sipped her coffee and looked out the window of the Dunbarton living room onto a Central Park that was completely cloaked in white. Which was the way it should always be on Christmas morning. The way it would be every morning, if she had her way, since she would forever associate snow with the first time she and Grant made love. Of course, she'd also think about him whenever she saw stars in the sky. And whenever she saw Christmas cupcakes. And fish. And chambered nautiluses...nautili...those macabre floaty things. And—

Well, suffice it to say she'd think about Grant a lot. Pretty much all the time. Since they would have so much time now that they had *both* abandoned their workaholic ways. Clara had even closed the bakery for the week between Christmas Eve and New Year's Day—with full pay for everyone—so that she and Hank could spend the holiday here in New York with family. It was the least she could do in light of Grant's giving up his position at Dunbarton Industries to ensure his own happiness. Learning how to let herself be happy was, hands down, the nicest gift she'd ever received for Christmas.

She turned to look at the pile of unopened packages under the tree behind the dozens of toys Santa had left for Hank. She didn't care what was in any of those boxes. Nothing could be better than what she'd already been given this year. Even so, she couldn't wait to open them. Just looking at them made her feel like… Well, like a kid at Christmas. Grant wasn't the only one who'd needed to get in touch with his inner child. Clara had needed to do more of that, too. Because she wanted to give that child the kind of Christmas she'd never had as a kid. And from here on out, she would.

True to her baker's hours, Clara had woken before everyone else. So the coffee was made, cinnamon buns and gingerbread were warming in the oven and a fire was crackling in the fireplace. She was still in her pajamas—the red flannel ones with snowflakes, identical to Hank's, which was a Christmas tradition for the two of them—and planned to stay in them all day. That was a Christmas tradition she and Hank had created, too, one she would introduce to the Dunbartons along with the handful of others she and her son had forged. They'd go nicely with the Dunbarton traditions, especially now that Grant and Francesca were planning to return to the ones they'd embraced when Grant was a child. Hence the cinnamon buns and gingerbread warming in the oven, something Grant had told her they'd always had for breakfast on Christmas morning when he was young.

As if conjured by her thoughts of him, he strode into the living room with a cup of coffee in one hand and a hunk of gingerbread in the other. He was still disheveled from sleep in dark green-and-gray-striped pajama bottoms and a gray T-shirt. Next year, he and Francesca would be in red flannel with snowflakes, too. This family was going to be so obnoxiously sweet in their Christmas clichés that they would gag a cotton candy factory. Because they all had a lot of time to make up for.

Grant smiled when he saw her, then held up the gingerbread. "I couldn't wait for breakfast. It smelled so good. Just like Christmas."

Clara smiled, too. "The best Christmas ever."

"How do you know?" he asked. "It's barely started."

"Doesn't matter," she told him. "I'm with you. That makes it the best Christmas ever."

He seemed to suddenly remember something, because he hurried to the end table and placed his coffee and gingerbread there, then headed for the tree and began sorting through the gifts.

"While it's just you and me," he said, "I want you to open your present. Well, one of them," he amended. "This one," he added when he located a small square box wrapped in shiny green paper.

"Okay, but you have to open one from me, too," she told him as she moved toward the tree to look for the one she wanted. She found it quickly, flat and rectangular and wrapped in bright blue. Like the ocean, she'd thought when she saw the paper. The perfect color.

For a moment, each of them knelt on the floor by the tree, clutching the packages they'd picked out for the other, knowing this first official sharing of Christmas gifts was a precedent for them both. She and Grant were family now. Not just through their ties to Hank. But through their ties to each other. Family ties didn't have to be blood ties. They didn't even have to be matrimonial ties. They just had to be love ties. And even if neither of them had said the actual words yet, she and Grant definitely had those.

As if decided upon in their mutual silence, they each thrust their present at the other. Then, as excited as children, they began to tear the paper to shreds.

Grant finished first, opening the box to reveal a trio of coloring books Clara had bought him at the New York Aquarium, along with a box of twenty-four crayons. At first she feared he was disappointed, because he just looked at them without touching them, not even to see what other books were under the one on top, which was called *Under the Sea* and was the most generic of them. She really wanted him to see the one on the bottom, called *I Am a Cephalopod*, because that was the one she knew he'd love most.

"Are there not enough crayons?" she asked. "I mean, I almost got the sixty-four count, but that just seemed so ostentatious, and I—"

"It's perfect, Clara," he said. When he looked up, his expression was absolutely sublime. "The twenty-four pack has Blue Green, which is what I always colored the ocean. And there's Red Orange for the firemouth cichlid. And Brown for the nautilus. You've given me everything I could ever need. Everything I could ever want."

She smiled at that. It was all she could ask a gift to do.

"Now finish opening yours," he told her.

She looked at the box in her lap, now completely freed of its wrappings. It was plain white, with no logo to give her a hint as to what it might be. Carefully, she pulled off the top. Beneath it was a crush of glittery tissue paper. She withdrew that, then caught her breath at what lay under it. A Christmas ornament. Rudolph the Red-Nosed Reindeer. Plastic with chipped paint and a red nail polish nose and a gigantic lump of dried glue on one leg. Her eyes filled with tears as she lifted it from its tissue paper bed, as carefully and reverently as she would have held the Hope Diamond.

"I can't believe you found this," she said. "Where...? How...?"

He grinned. "Would you believe...the magic of Christmas?"

She grinned back. "Gee, I don't know. Something like this would take an awful lot of magic."

"Then how about a friend who's a high-ranking member of the NYPD and married to a social worker who knew who to call to ask about your file in Georgia and find out who you were living with when you were about eight years old?"

Clara shook her head in astonishment. "I can't believe you went to all that trouble."

"It was no trouble," he said. "Anything to make you as happy as you've made me."

"It doesn't take a Christmas ornament to do that," Clara told him.

"Maybe not," he said. "But if it makes you happy..."

"Very happy," she assured him.

"Then I'm happy, too."

Clara was leaning in to give him a kiss when she heard the patter of Hank's feet slapping down the hall toward them, followed by an admonishment from Francesca to *Wait for me!* Hah. Not likely. No kid could wait on Christmas morning. Not for anything.

"You started without me!" Hank exclaimed when he saw the evidence of opened presents littering the floor between her and Grant.

But he was quickly sidetracked when he saw the toys from Santa scattered about and headed immediately for those. Francesca dove in right behind him, her merriment rivaling his.

Clara and Grant looked at each other. And she knew in that moment that they were both thinking exactly the same thing. Yes, they had started without Hank this morning. But that was just the point. They had *started.* Finally. They had started living. They had started loving. They had started feeling happy. Really happy. The kind of happy that only came in knowing they were exactly where they wanted and needed to be. Exactly where they belonged.

"Merry Christmas, Clara," Grant said softly. "I love you."

Had she just been thinking that learning how to let herself be happy was the nicest Christmas present she'd ever received? Gee, she'd been mistaken. That was the second best. The first was sitting right across from her, telling her he loved her.

"Merry Christmas, Grant," she replied just as quietly. "I love you, too."

And amid the ringing of laughter and the aroma of evergreen and gingerbread, closing their fingers over remnants of their childhood that now brought joy instead of sadness, Clara and Grant shared another kiss. The first of many they would share that day, Clara was certain. The first of many they would share in life. Because that was what life was. Sharing. Living. Loving. From one Christmas morning to the next.

Epilogue

Clara was dabbing a smile on the last of two dozen dolphin cookies when the bell over the entrance to Cairns, Australia's Bread & Buttercream rang for what she hoped was the last time that day. Not that she didn't love every customer who came into her new digs in Clifton Beach, but with the grand opening just over and Christmas only a few weeks away, the bakery had been super busy. Not to mention she had to pick up Hank from Camp Australia for first graders—um, she meant year one students—in… She glanced at the clock. Yikes! Less than an hour! Where had the day gone?

She placed the dolphin on a rack with the rest of his pod to let the glaze dry, setting aside a basket of papayas that she and Hank had picked fresh from a tree in their backyard yesterday evening, before they'd stopped to catch fireflies in a jar. Then she wiped her powdered sugar–dusted hands on her white apron, which was easier now with the soft curve of her baby bump rising up to greet them.

She let her hands linger over the slight swell. She was barely four months along, but had already outgrown some of the maternity clothes that were supposed to last till her third trimester. Her ob-gyn had said they were going to do an ultrasound next visit to check for twins, something that still made Clara a little woozy. Still, Hank was already jazzed about the prospect of having one little brother or sister. Two might very well make him Big Brother of the Year.

She heard her salesclerk Merindah greet someone out in the shop with a happy hello, then Grant's voice replying. Clara smiled. He always took off from work early on Friday to meet her at the bakery so they could pick up their son together and get an early start on the weekend. He'd been busy, too, the past few months, getting his nonprofit, A Drop in the Ocean, off the ground. Okay, so it wasn't as catchy as KOOK, but it still had a certain whimsy. And already, it was making a difference. The organization employed more than two dozen people here and would be helping to preserve ecosystems from the Great Barrier Reef to Nauru and the Cook Islands. For starters. Although Grant had chosen Cairns for the main headquarters, he wanted to open satellite sites for A Drop in the Ocean all over the world. He'd funded much of its endowment with his own money, but thanks to his contacts in the business world, he had regular—and substantial—donors from some pretty major sources. Yes, he was the organization's CEO. But he wasn't relentless. He wasn't joyless. He wasn't a workaholic. He'd taken his dream and run with it. The same way Clara had. But they both made sure those dreams included time for each other.

After ensuring that Merindah and Clara's part-timer, Susan, didn't need anything before the bakery's close, she kissed her husband and asked him about his day.

"It was busy," he said.

But it was a good busy, Clara could tell. In the three years she'd known him, she'd never seen Grant look happier than he had since their move here. His skin was burnished from his time outdoors, and his hair was longer and less tidy than it had been when she first met him. He lived in Hawaiian shirts and cargo shorts these days, and he drove an old, army-green Range Rover—the kind he'd said he always wanted to have when he was a kid. They lived in a big house on the beach, surrounded by palm and mango trees, where they were occasionally visited by dolphins and goannas. The night sky was amazing, completely different from the one Hank had learned when he was little. And there were a million things to explore. It was a better life than Clara could have ever imagined for her son. Or for Grant. Or for herself.

She'd never been happier, either.

Grant helped her into the Ranger Rover, and after she was buckled in, he placed his hand gently over her swollen abdomen. "Think there are two in there?" he asked.

"Could be," Clara told him. She suspected there were, and her doctor had all but said she thought there were, too, but they wouldn't know for sure until after the ultrasound. "Would you be okay with that?"

He grinned. "Totally. And Mom would be beside herself. She's sure if we just have enough kids, one of them is bound to inherit the CEO gene, and then she can train them to follow in their grandmother's footsteps."

Clara grinned, too. "So she's coming next week, right?"

He nodded. "She gave herself the rest of December off, flying back to New York the day after New Year's."

Clara looked up at the sun and swiped at a trickle of perspiration on her neck. "Guess we can forget about white Christmases here." Funny, though, how that didn't bother her as much as she might have thought it would.

Grant closed the door of the Range Rover and, through the open window, told her, "We don't need snow to make it Christmas."

And that was certainly true. They could make it Christmas anywhere. And everywhere. And not just at Christmastime, either. All it took was knowing they were together. Exactly where they wanted to be. Exactly where they needed to be. Exactly where they belonged.

* * * * *

RECLAIMED BY THE RANCHER

Janice Maynard

One

Not much rattled Jeff Hartley. At twenty-nine, he owned and operated the family ranch where he had grown up during a near-idyllic childhood. His parents had taken early retirement back in the spring and had headed off to a condo on Galveston Bay, leaving their only son to carry on the tradition.

Jeff was a full member of the prestigious Texas Cattleman's Club, a venerable establishment where the movers and shakers of Royal, Texas, met to shoot the breeze and oftentimes conduct business. Jeff prided himself on being mature, efficient, easygoing and practical.

But when he opened his door on a warm October afternoon and saw Lucy Peyton standing on his front porch, it felt as if a bull had kicked him in the chest. First there was the dearth of oxygen, a damned scary feeling. Then the pain set in. After that, he had the impulse to flee before the bull could take another shot.

He stared at his visitor, his gaze as level and dispassionate as he could make it. "I plan to vote Democrat this year. I don't need any magazine subscriptions. And I already have a church home," he said. "But thanks for stopping by."

He almost had the door closed before she spoke. "Jeff. Please. I need to talk to you."

Damn it. How could a woman say his name—one measly syllable—and make his insides go all wonky? Her voice was every bit the same as he remembered. Soft and husky…as if she were on the verge of laryngitis. Or perhaps about to offer some lucky man naughty, unspeakable pleasure in the bedroom.

The sound of eight words, no matter how urgently spoken, shouldn't have made him weak in the knees.

Her looks hadn't changed, either, though she was a bit thinner than he remembered. Her dark brown hair, all one length but parted on the side, brushed her shoulders. Hazel eyes still reminded him of an autumn pond filled with fallen leaves.

She was tall, at least five-eight…and though she was athletic and graceful, she had plenty of curves to add interest to the map. Some of those curves still kept him awake on dark, troubled nights.

"Unless you're here to apologize," he said, his words deliberately curt, "I don't think we have anything to talk about."

When she shoved her shoulder against the door, he had to step back or risk hurting her. Even so, he planted himself in the doorway, drawing a metaphorical line in the sand.

Her eyes widened, even as they flashed with temper. "How *dare* you try to play the wronged party, you *lying, cheating, sonofa—*"

Either she ran out of adjectives, or she suddenly realized that insulting a man was no way to gain entry into his home.

He lifted an eyebrow. "You were saying?"

His mild tone seemed to enrage her further, though to her credit, she managed to swallow whatever additional words trembled on her tongue. Was it bad of him to remember that small pink tongue wetting his— Oh, hell. Now *he* was the one who pulled up short. Nothing stood to be gained by indulging in a sentimental stroll down memory lane.

No tongues. No nothing.

She licked her lips and took a deep, visible breath. "Samson Oil is trying to buy the Peyton ranch."

Two

Lucy was diabetic; she'd been diagnosed as a twelve-year-old. If she didn't take her insulin, she sometimes got the shakes. But nothing like this. Facing the man she had come to see made her tremble from head to toe. And she couldn't seem to stop. No amount of medicine in the world was ever going to cure her fascination with the ornery, immoral, two-faced, spectacularly handsome Jeff Hartley.

At the moment, however, he was her only hope.

"May I come in?" she asked, trying not to notice the way he smelled of leather and lime and warm male skin.

Jeff stared at her long enough to make her think he might actually say no. In the end, however, gentlemanly manners won out. "Ten minutes," he said gruffly. "I have plans later."

If he meant to wound her, his barb was successful… though she would never give him the satisfaction of knowing for sure. As they navigated the few steps into his living room and sat down, she found herself swamped with memories. This old farmhouse dated back three generations. It had been lovingly cared for and well preserved.

For one brief second, everything came crashing back: the hours she had spent in this bright, cheerful home, the master bedroom upstairs with the queen-size mattress and double-wedding-ring quilt, the bed Jeff had complained was too small for his six-foot-two frame…

She didn't want to remember. Not at all. Not even the spot in this very room where Jeff Hartley had gone down on one knee and offered her a ring and his heart.

Dredging up reserves of audacity and courage, she ignored the past and cut to the chase. "My cousin is trying to sell his land to Samson Oil." Recently, the outsider company had begun buying up acreage in Royal, Texas, at an alarming rate.

Jeff sat back in a leather armchair and hitched one ankle across the opposite knee, drawing attention to his feet. "Is it a fair offer?"

Nobody Lucy had ever known wore scuffed, hand-tooled cowboy boots as well as Jeff Hartley. At one time she wondered if he slept in the damned things. But then came that memorable evening when he showed her how a woman could take off a man's boots at the end of the day…

Her face heated. She jerked her thoughts back to the present. "More than fair. But that's not the point. The property has been in the Peyton family for almost a century. The farmland has contributed to Maverick County's food supply for decades. Equally important—the wildlife preserve was my grandfather's baby. Samson Oil will ruin everything."

"Why does Kenny want to sell?"

"He's sick of farming. He swears there's nothing for him in Royal anymore. He's decided to move to LA and try for an acting career. He pointed out that I sold most of my share to him, left for college and then stayed away. He wants his chance. But he needs cash."

"And this is my problem, how?"

Three

Lucy bit her lip until she tasted blood in her mouth. She couldn't afford to let Jeff goad her into losing her temper. It had happened far too easily on his front porch a moment ago. Her only focus right now should be on getting what she needed to stop a bad, bad decision.

It might have helped if Jeff had gotten old and fat in the past two years. But unfortunately, he looked better than ever. Dark blond hair in need of a trim. Piercing green eyes, definitely on the hostile side. And a long, lean body and lazy gait that made grown women sigh with delight whenever he sauntered by.

"I need you to loan me twenty thousand dollars," she blurted out. "The farm is self-supporting, but Kenny doesn't have a lot of liquid assets. He may be bluffing. Even if he's serious, though, twenty grand will get him off my back and send him on his way. He thinks the only choice he has for coming up with relocation funds is to unload the farm, but I'm trying to give him another option."

"What will happen to the farm when he goes to the West Coast?"

It was a good question. And one she had wrestled with ever since Kenny told her he wanted to leave town. "I suppose I'll have to come back to Royal and take over. At least until Kenny crashes and burns in California and decides to return home."

"You don't have much faith in him, do you?"

She shrugged. "Our fathers were brothers. So we share DNA. But Kenny has always had a problem with focus. Six months ago he wanted to go to vet school. Six months before that he was studying to take the LSAT."

"But you already have a career…right? As a physical trainer? In Austin? That fancy master's degree you earned in sports medicine won't do you much good out on the farm." He didn't even bother to hide the sarcasm.

She wanted to squirm, but she concentrated on breathing in and breathing out, relaxing her muscles one set at a time. "Fortunately, mine is the kind of job that's in demand. I'm sure they won't hold my exact position, but there will be plenty of similar spots when I go back."

"How long do you think you'll have to stay here in Royal?"

"A few months. A year at the most. Will you loan me the money, or not?"

Jeff scowled. "You've got a lot of balls coming to me for help, Lucy."

"You *owe* me," she said firmly. "And you know it." This man…this beautiful, rugged snake of a man had been responsible for the second worst day of her life.

He sat up and leaned forward, resting his elbows on

his knees. His veneer of calm peeled away, leaving a male who was a little bit frightening. Dark emerald eyes judged her and found her wanting. “I don’t *owe* you a single damn thing. You’re the one who walked out on our wedding and made me a laughingstock in Royal.”

She jumped to her feet, heart pounding. Lord, he made her mad. “Because I caught you at our rehearsal dinner kissing the maid of honor,” she yelled.

Four

Something about Lucy's meltdown actually made Jeff feel a little bit better about this confrontation. At least she wasn't indifferent.

"Sit down, Lucy," he said firmly. "If money is going to change hands, I have two conditions."

She did sit, but the motion looked involuntary…as if her knees gave out. "Conditions?"

"It's a lot of money. And besides, why ask me? Me, of all people?"

"You're rich," she said bluntly, her stormy gaze daring him to disagree.

It was true. His bank account was healthy. And sadly, Lucy had no family to turn to, other than her cousin. Lucy's parents and Kenny's had been killed in a boating accident eight years ago. Because of that tragedy, Lucy had a closer relationship with her cousin than one might expect. They were more like siblings, really.

"If my bottom line is good, it's partly because I don't toss money out the window on a whim."

"It wouldn't be a whim, Jeff. I know the way you think. This thing with Samson Oil is surely eating away at you. *Outsiders.* Taking over land that represents the history of Royal. And then doing God knows what with it. Drilling for oil that isn't there. Selling off the dud acres. Shopping malls. Big box stores. Admit it. The thought makes you shudder. You have to be suspicious about why a mysterious oil company is suddenly trying to buy land that was checked for oil years ago."

That was the problem with old girlfriends. They knew a man's weaknesses. "You're not wrong," he said slowly, taken aback that she had pegged him so well. "But in that case, why wouldn't I buy Kenny's land outright? And make sure that it retains its original purpose?"

"Because it's not the honorable thing to do. Kenny will see the light one day soon. And he would be devastated to come back to Royal and have nothing. Besides, that would be a whole lot more money. Twenty thousand is chicken feed to you."

Jeff grimaced. "You must know some damn fine chickens."

Perhaps she understood him better than he wanted to admit, because after laying out her case, she sat quietly, giving him time to sort through the possibilities. Lucy stared at him with hazel eyes that reflected wariness and a hint of grief.

He felt the grief, too. Had wallowed in it for weeks. But a man had to move on with his life. At one time, he'd been absolutely sure he would grow old with this woman. Now he could barely look at her.

"I need to think about it," he said.

Lucy's temper fired again. "Since when do you have trouble making decisions?" Her hands twisted together in her lap as if she wanted to wrap them around his neck.

"Don't push me, Lucy." He scowled at her. "I'll pick you up out at the farm at five. We'll have dinner, and I'll give you my answer."

Her throat worked. "I don't want to be seen with you."

Five

The barb wasn't unexpected, but it took Jeff's breath momentarily. "The feeling is mutual," he growled. "I'll make reservations in Midland. We'll discuss my terms."

"But that's fifty miles away."

Her visible dismay gave him deep masculine satisfaction. It was time for some payback. Lucy deserved to twist in the wind for what she had done to him. A man's pride was everything.

"Take it or leave it," he said, the words curt.

"I thought you had plans later."

"You let me worry about my calendar, sweetheart."

He watched her flinch at his overt sarcasm. For a moment, he was ashamed of baiting her. But he shored up his anger. Lucy deserved his antagonism and more.

The silence grew in length and breadth, thick with unspoken emotions. If he listened hard enough, he thought he might even be able to hear the rapid beat of her heart. Like a defenseless animal trapped in a cage of its own making.

"Lucy?" He lifted an eyebrow. "I don't have all day."

"You could write me a check this instant," she protested. "Why make me jump through hoops?"

"Maybe because I can."

He was being a bastard. He knew it. And by the look on Lucy's face, she knew it, as well. But the opportunity to make her bend to his will was irresistible.

The fact that each of them could still elicit strong emotions from the other should have been a red flag. But then again, that was the story of their relationship. Though he and Lucy had grown up in the same town, they hadn't really known each other. Not until she'd come home to Royal for a lengthy visit after college graduation.

Lucy's parents had been dead by then. Instead of bunking with her cousin Kenny, Lucy had stayed with her childhood friend and college roommate, Kirsten. One of Kirsten's friends had thrown a hello-to-summer bash, and that's where Jeff had met the luscious Lucy.

He still remembered the moment she'd walked into the room. It was a case of instant lust…at least on his part. She was exactly the kind of woman he liked… tall, confident, and with a wicked sense of humor. The two of them had found a private corner and flirted for three hours.

A week later, they'd ended up in bed together.

Unfortunately, their whirlwind courtship and speedy five-month trip to the altar had ended in disaster. Ironically, if they had followed through with their wedding, two days from now would have been their anniversary.

Did Lucy realize the bizarre coincidence?

She stood up and walked to the foyer. "I have to

go." The words were tossed over her shoulder, as if she couldn't wait to get out of his house.

He shrugged and followed her, putting a hand high on the door to keep her from escaping. "I don't want to make a trip out to the farm for nothing. So don't try standing me up. If you want the money, you'll get it on my terms or not at all."

Six

Lucy hurried to her car, heartsick and panicked. Why had she ever thought she could appeal to Jeff Hartley's sense of right and wrong? The man was a scoundrel. She was so angry with herself...angry for approaching him in the first place, and even angrier that apparently she was still desperately in love with him...despite everything he had done.

During the past two years, she had firmly purged her emotional system of memories connected to Jeff Hartley. Never once did she think of the way his arms pulled her tight against his broad chest. Or the silkiness of his always rumpled hair. At night in bed, she surely didn't remember how wonderful it was to feel him slide on top of her and into her, their breath mingling in ragged gasps and groans of pleasure.

Stupid man. She parked haphazardly at the farm and went in search of her cousin. She found him in the barn repairing a harness.

Kenny looked up when she entered. "Hey, Luce. What's up?"

She plopped down on a bale of hay. "How much would it take for you not to sell the land?"

He frowned. "What do you mean? Are you trying to buy it for yourself?"

"Gosh, no. I'd be a terrible farmer. But I have a gut feeling you'll change your mind down the road. And I'm willing to keep things running while you sow your wild oats. So I'm asking…would twenty grand be enough to bankroll your move to LA and get you started? It would be a loan. You'd have to pay back half eventually, and I'll pay back the other half as a thank-you for not letting go of Peyton land."

The frown grew deeper. "A loan from whom?"

Kenny might pretend to be a goofball when it suited him, but the boy was smart…and he knew his grammar.

"From a friend of mine," she said. "No big deal."

Kenny perched on the bale of hay beside hers and put an arm around her shoulders. "What have you done, Luce?"

She sniffed, trying not to cry. "Made a deal with the devil?"

"Are you asking me or telling me?"

Kenny was two years younger than she was. Most of the time she felt like his mother. But for the moment, it was nice to have someone to lean on. "I think Jeff Hartley is going to loan it to me."

"Hell, no." Kenny jumped to his feet, raking both hands through his hair agitatedly. "The man cheated on you and broke your heart. I won't take his money. We'll think of something else. Or I'll convince you it's okay to sell the farm."

"You'll never convince me of that. What if being an actor doesn't pan out?"

"Do you realize how patronizing you sound, Luce? No offense, but what I want to do is more serious than *sowing wild oats*."

She rubbed her temples with her fingertips. "I shouldn't have said that. I'm sorry."

After a few moments, he went back to repairing the harness. "Why did you go to Jeff, Lucy? Why him?"

Bowing her head, she let the tears fall. "The day after tomorrow would have been our wedding anniversary. Jeff Hartley still owes me for that."

Seven

Jeff made arrangements to have the Hartley Ranch covered, personnel wise, in the event that he didn't return from Midland right away. There was no reason in the world to think that he and Lucy might end up in bed together, but he was a planner. A former Boy Scout. Preparation was second nature to him.

As he went about his business, his mind raced on a far more intimate track. Lucy had betrayed the wedding vows she and Jeff had both written. Before they'd ever made it to the altar. And yet she thought Jeff was the one at fault. Even from the perspective of two years down the road, he was still angry about that.

At four o'clock, he showered and quickly packed a bag. He traveled often for cattle shows and other business-related trips, so he was accustomed to the drill. Then he went online and ordered a variety of items and had them delivered to his favorite hotel.

When he was satisfied that his plans were perfectly in order, he loaded the car, stopped by the bank, and then drove out to the farm. There was at least a fifty-fifty chance Lucy would shut the door in his face. But he was convinced her request for a loan was legit. In order to get the cash, she had to go along with his wishes.

Unfortunately, Kenny answered the door. And he was spoiling for a fight.

Jeff had spent his entire life in Texas. He was no stranger to brawls and the occasional testosterone overload. But if he had plans for himself and Lucy, first he had to get past her gatekeeper. He held up his hands in the universal gesture for noncombative behavior. "I come in peace, big guy."

"Luce never should have asked you for the money. I can manage on my own."

"In LA? I don't think so. Not without liquidating your assets. And that will break your cousin's heart. Is that really what you want to do?"

"You're hardly the man to talk about breaking Lucy's heart." But it was said without heat. As if Kenny understood that more was at stake here than his would-be career.

"Where is she?" Jeff asked. "We need to go."

"I think she was on the phone, but she'll be out soon. Though I sure as hell don't know why."

"Lucy and I have some unfinished business from two years ago. It's time to settle a few scores."

Kenny blanched. "I don't want to be in the middle of this."

"Too late. You shouldn't have tried to sell your land

to Samson Oil. And besides, Lucy came to me…not the other way around. What does that tell you?"

Kenny bristled. "It tells me that my cousin cares about me. I have no idea what it says about you."

Eight

Lucy stood just out of sight in the hallway and listened to the two men argue. Strangely, there was not much real anger in the exchange. At one time, Kenny and Jeff had been good friends. Kenny was supposed to walk Lucy down the aisle and hand her over to the rancher who had swept her off her feet. But that moment never happened.

Lucy cleared her throat and eased past Kenny to step onto the porch. “Don’t worry if I’m late,” she said.

Kenny tugged her wrist and leaned in to kiss her on the cheek. “Text me and let me know your plans. So I don’t worry.”

His droll attempt to play mother hen made her smile. “Very funny. But yes… I’ll be in touch.”

At last she had to face Jeff. He stood a few feet away, his expression inscrutable. In a dark tailored suit, with a crisp white dress shirt and blue patterned tie, he looked like a man in charge of his domain. A light breeze ruffled his hair.

His sharp, intimate gaze scanned her from head to toe. "Let's go" was all he said.

Lucy sighed inwardly. So much for her sexy black cocktail dress with spaghetti straps. The daring bodice showcased her cleavage nicely. Big surly rancher barely seemed to notice.

They descended the steps side by side, Jeff's hand on her elbow. He helped her into the car, closed her door and went around to slide into the driver's seat. The car was not one she remembered. But it had all the bells and whistles. It smelled of leather and even more faintly, the essence of the man himself.

For the first ten miles silence reigned. Pastures of cattle whizzed by outside the window, their existence so commonplace, Lucy couldn't pretend a deep interest in the scenery. Instead, she kicked off her shoes, curled her legs beneath her, and leaned forward to turn on the satellite radio.

"Do you mind?" she asked.

Jeff shot her a glance. "Does being alone with me make you nervous, Lucy?"

"Of course not." Her hand hovered over the knob. More than anything else, she wanted music to fill the awkward silence. But if Jeff saw that as a sign of weakness, then she wouldn't do it.

She sat back, biting her bottom lip. Now the silence was worse. Before, they had simply been two near strangers riding down the road. Jeff's deliberately provocative question set her nerves on edge.

"While we're on our way," she said, "why don't you tell me what these conditions are? The ones I have to agree to so you'll loan me the money?"

Jeff didn't answer her question. "I'm curious. Why doesn't Kenny go out and get his own loan?"

"He's shoveled everything he has back into the farm. His credit's maxed out. Besides, his solution is selling to Samson Oil. I explained that."

"True. You did."

"So tell me, Jeff. What do you want from me?"

Nine

What do you want from me? Lucy's frustrated question was one Jeff would have been glad to answer. In detail. Slowly. All night. But first there were hurdles to jump.

Though he kept his hands on the wheel and his eyes on the road, he had already memorized every nuance of his companion's appearance. Everything from her sexy black high heels all the way up to her sleek and shiny hair tucked behind one ear.

Her black cocktail dress, at first glance, was entirely appropriate for dinner in the big city. But damned if he wasn't going to have the urge to take off his jacket and wrap her up in it. He didn't want other men looking at her.

He felt possessive, which was ridiculous, because Lucy was definitely her own woman. If she chose to prance stark naked down Main Street, he couldn't stop her. So maybe he needed to take a different tack entirely. Instead of bossing her around, perhaps he should use another very enjoyable means of communication.

Right now, she was a hen with ruffled feathers. He had upset her already. The truth was, he didn't care. He'd rather have anger from Lucy than outright indifference.

He could work with anger.

"We'll talk about the specifics over dinner, Lucy. Why don't you relax and tell me about your work in Austin."

His diversion worked for the next half hour. In his peripheral vision, he watched as Lucy's body language went from tense and guarded to normal. Or at least as normal as it could be given the history between them.

Later, when he pulled up in front of the luxury hotel in the heart of the city, Lucy shot him a sharp-eyed glance.

He took her elbow and led her inside. "The restaurant here is phenomenal," he said. "I think you'll enjoy it."

Over appetizers and drinks, Lucy thawed further. "So far, I'm impressed. I forgot to eat lunch today, so I was starving."

Jeff was hungry, too, but he barely tasted the food. He was gambling a hell of a lot on the outcome of this encounter.

They ordered the works…filet and lobster. With spinach salad and crusty rolls. Clearly, Lucy enjoyed her meal. *He* enjoyed the fact that she didn't fuss about calories and instead ate with enthusiasm.

Good food prepared from fresh ingredients was a sensual experience. It tapped into some of the same pleasure centers as lovemaking. It was hard to bicker under the influence of a really exceptional Chablis and a satisfying, special-occasion dinner.

That's what he was counting on…

Lucy declined dessert. Jeff did, as well. As they lingered over coffee, he could practically see her girding her loins for battle.

She stirred a single packet of sugar into her cup and sat back in her chair, eyeing him steadily. "Enough stalling, Jeff. I've come here with you for dinner, which was amazing, I might add. But I need to have your answer. Will you loan me the money, and what are your conditions?"

Ten

Lucy was braced for bad news. It was entirely possible that Jeff had brought her here—wined and dined her—in order to let her down gently. To give her an outright no.

Watching him take a sip of coffee was only one of many mistakes she had made tonight. When his lips made contact with the rim of his thin china cup, she was almost sure the world stood still for a split second. The man had the most amazing mouth. Firm lips that could caress a woman's breast or kiss her senseless in the space of a heartbeat.

Though it had been two long years, Lucy still remembered the taste of his tongue on hers.

"Jeff?" She heard the impatience in her voice. "I asked you a question."

He nodded slowly. "Okay. Hear me out before you run screaming from the room."

Her nape prickled. "I don't understand."

Leaning toward her, he rested his forearms on the table, hands clasped in front of him. His dark gaze captured hers like a mesmerist. "When you walked out the night before our wedding, we never had closure. I went from being almost married to drastically single so fast it's a wonder I didn't get whiplash."

"What's your point?" Her throat was tight.

"Divorced couples end up back in bed together all the time. Lovers break up and hook up and break up again. I'm curious to see if you and I still have a spark."

Hyperventilation threatened. "We can talk about that later." *Much later.* "You said you had two conditions. What are they?" For the first time tonight, she caught a glimpse of something in his eyes. Was it pain? Or vulnerability? Not likely.

He shrugged. "I want you to ask Kirsten to tell you what really happened that night."

"I don't need to talk to Kirsten. I'm not blind. I saw everything. You kissed her and she kissed you back. Both of you betrayed me. The truth is, Kirsten and I have barely spoken since that night. She has shut me out. I think she's embarrassed that she didn't stop you."

"And you really believe that?"

His tone wasn't sarcastic. If anything, the words were wistful, cajoling. She'd spent two horrid years wondering why the man who professed to love her madly had been such a jerk. Or why Kirsten, her best friend, hadn't punched Jeff in the stomach. She had seen Kirsten's face when Lucy caught them. The other woman had looked shattered. But her arms had definitely been twined about Jeff's neck.

"I don't know what to believe anymore," she muttered. Jeff hadn't dated anyone at all in the last twenty-four months according to Royal's gossipy grapevine. He was a young, virile man in his prime. If he was such a lying, cheating scoundrel, why hadn't he been out on the town with a dozen women in the interim? "And if I do go talk to Kirsten about what happened? That's it? What about the other requirement?"

Those chiseled lips curved upward in a smile that made her spine tighten and her stomach curl. "I'd like the two of us to go upstairs and spend the night together."

Eleven

Go upstairs and spend the night together.

His words echoed in her brain like tiny pinballs. "You mean sex?"

Jeff laughed out loud, but it was gentle laughter, and his eyes were filled with warmth. "Yes, Lucy. Sex. I've missed you. I've missed us."

Oh, my...

What was a woman supposed to say to that kind of proposition? Especially when it sounded so very appealing. She cleared her throat. "If you're offering to pay me twenty thousand dollars to have sex with you, I think we could both get arrested."

His smile was enigmatic. "Let's not muddy the waters, then. I promise to give you the money for Kenny as long as you have a conversation with Kirsten." He reached across the table and took one of her hands in both of his. When he rubbed his thumb across her wrist, it was all she could do not to jerk away in a panic.

"Steady, Lucy." His grip tightened. "I think deep in your heart you know the truth. But you're afraid to face it. I understand that. Maybe it will take time. So for tonight, I'm not expecting you to make any sweeping declarations. I'm only asking if you'll be my lover again. One night. For closure. Unless you change your mind and decide you want more."

"Why would I do that?" she asked faintly, remembering all the evenings she had cried herself to sleep.

"You'll have to figure it out for yourself," he said. That same thumb rubbed back and forth across her knuckles.

She seized on one inescapable truth. "But I don't have anything with me to stay overnight," she said, grasping at straws. "And neither do you."

"I brought a bag," he replied calmly. "And I ordered a few items for a female companion. I believe you'll find I've thought of everything you need to be comfortable."

"And you don't think this is at all creepy?" With her free hand she picked up her water glass, intending to take a sip. But her fingers shook so much she set it back down immediately.

Jeff released her, his expression sober. "You're the one who came to see me, not the other way around. If you want me to take you home, all you have to do is say so. But I'm hoping you'll give us this one night to see if the spark is still there."

"Why are you doing this?" she whispered. He was breaking her heart all over again, and she was so damned afraid to trust him. Even worse, she was afraid to trust herself.

Jeff summoned the waiter and dealt with the check.

Moments later, the transaction was complete. Jeff stood and held out his hand. "I need your decision, Lucy." He was tall and sexy and clear-eyed in his resolve. "Shall we go, or shall we stay? It's up to you. It always has been."

Twelve

Jeff's heartbeat thundered in his chest. He wasn't usually much of a gambler, but he was betting on a future that, at the moment, didn't exist.

It was a thousand years before Lucy slid her small hand into his bigger one. "Yes," she said. The word was barely audible.

He led her among the crowded tables and out into the hotel foyer. After tucking her into an elegant wing-back chair, he brushed a finger across her cheek. "Stay here. I won't be long."

Perhaps the desk clerk thought him a tad weird. Jeff could barely register for glancing back over his shoulder to see if Lucy had bolted. But all was well. She had her phone in her hand and was apparently checking messages.

When he had the key, he went back for her. "Ready?"

Her face was pale when she looked up at him. But she smiled and rose to her feet. "Yes."

They shared an elevator with three other people. On the seventh floor, Jeff took Lucy's arm and steered her off. "This way," he said gruffly as he located their room number on the brass placard. They were at the end of the hall, far from the noise of the elevator and the ice machine.

He'd booked a suite. Inside the pleasantly neutral sitting room, he took off his jacket and tie. "Would you like more wine?" he asked.

Lucy hovered by the door. "No. Why do you want me to go talk to Kirsten?" Her eyes were huge…perhaps revealing distress over the shambles of their past.

He leaned against the arm of the sofa. "She was your friend from childhood. You and I had dated less than a year. As angry as I was with you, on some level I understood."

"Why were you angry with *me*?" she asked, her expression bewildered. "You were the one who cheated."

He didn't rise to the bait. "It's been two years, Lucy. Two long, frustrating years when you and I should have been starting our life together. Surely you've had time enough to figure it out by now."

"You didn't come after me." Her voice was small, the tone wounded.

Ah…there it was. The evidence of his own stupidity. "You're right about that. I let my pride get in the way. When you wouldn't take my calls, I wanted to make you grovel. But as it turns out, that was an abysmally arrogant and unproductive attitude on my part. I'm sorry I didn't follow you back to Austin. I should have. Maybe one good knock-down, drag-out fight would have cleared the air."

"And now...if I agree to go talk to Kirsten?"

He swallowed the last of his wine and set the glass aside. "I don't want to discuss Kirsten anymore. You and I are the only two people here in this suite. What I desperately need is make love to you."

Thirteen

Lucy sucked in a deep breath, her insides tumbling as they had the one and only time she rode the Tilt-A-Whirl at the county fair. On that occasion, she had tossed her cookies afterward.

Tonight was different. Tonight, the butterflies were all about anticipation and arousal and the rebirth of hope. Why else would she be here with Jeff Hartley?

She nodded, kicking off her shoes. "Yes." There were a million words she wanted to say to him, and not all of them kind. But for some reason, the only thing that mattered at this very moment was feeling the warmth of his skin beneath her fingers one more time.

She felt more emotionally bereft than brave, but she made her feet move...carrying her across the plush carpet until she stood face-to-face with Jeff. His gaze was stormy, his fists were clenched at his sides.

He stared into her eyes as if looking for something

he was afraid he wouldn't find. "God, you're beautiful," he said, his voice hoarse. "I thought I could put you out of my mind, but that was laughable. You've haunted every room in my house. Kiss me, Lucy."

With one of his strong arms around her back, binding her to him, she went up on her tiptoes and found his mouth with hers. The taste of him brought tears to sting her eyelids, but she blinked them back, wanting this moment to be about light and warmth and pleasure. He held her gently as he took everything she thought she knew and stripped it away, leaving only a yearning that was heart-deep and visceral.

She wanted to say something, but Jeff was a man possessed. He found the zipper at her back and lowered it with one smooth move. Then he shimmied the garment down her body and held her arm as she stepped out of the small heap of fabric.

Beneath the dress, she wore lacy underthings. Jeff didn't pause to admire them. The lingerie went the way of the crumpled dress.

Suddenly, she realized that she was completely naked, and her would-be lover was staring. Hotly. Glassy-eyed. As if he'd been struck in the head and was seeing stars.

She crossed her arms over strategic areas and scowled. "Take off your clothes, Mr. Hartley. This show works both ways."

If the situation hadn't been so emotionally fraught, she might have chuckled when Jeff dragged his shirt, still half-buttoned, over his head. His pants and socks and shoes were next in the frenzied disrobing.

Underneath, he wore snug-fitting black boxers that strained to contain his arousal. Suddenly, she felt shy and afraid and clueless. Had she ever really known this man at all?

He didn't give her time for second thoughts. "We'll be more comfortable on the bed," he promised, scooping her up and carrying her through the adjacent doorway. She barely noticed the furnishings or the color scheme. Her gaze was locked on Jeff's face.

His cheekbones were slashed with color. His eyes glittered with lust. "You're mine, Lucy."

Fourteen

The bottom dropped out of her stomach. It was as simple as that. Even if he hadn't said the words, she would have felt his deep conviction in the way he moved his hands over her body.

He still wore his underwear, maybe to keep things from rushing along too rapidly. He was tanned all over from his days of working in the hot sun. His chest was a work of art, sleekly muscled…lightly dusted with golden hair.

Even as she took in the magnificence that was Jeff Hartley, she couldn't help but question his motives. As a rancher and a member of the Texas Cattleman's Club in Royal, he was a well-respected member of the community. Had his reputation suffered when she walked out on him? Was there a part of him that wanted revenge?

He loomed over her on one elbow, his emerald eyes darker than normal, his forehead damp, his skin hot.

It was all she could do to be still and let him map her curves like a blind man. Need rose, hot and tormenting, between her clenched thighs.

How could she want him so desperately while knowing full well there were serious unresolved issues between them? "Jeff," she whispered, not really knowing what to say. "Please…" Despite what her head told her, her heart and her body were in control.

It was as if they had never been apart. He rolled her to her stomach and moved aside a swath of her hair to kiss the nape of her neck. The press of his lips against sensitive skin sent sparkles of sensation all down to her feet.

When he nibbled his way along her spine, her hands grabbed the sheets. He lay heavy against her, his big body weighing her down deliciously.

At last she felt him move away. He scrambled out of his boxers and rolled her to face him once again. She let her arms fall lax above her head, enjoying the way his avid gaze scoured her from head to toe.

It had been two years since she had seen him naked… two years since she had seen him at all. Beginning with what would have been their wedding morning, he had phoned her every single day for a week. Each one of those times she had let his call go to voice mail, telling herself he should have had the guts to face her in person.

Had she wronged him grievously? In her blind hurt, had she rushed to judgment? The enormity of the question made her head spin.

For weeks and months, she had wallowed in her self-righteous anger, calling Jeff Hartley every dirty name in the book, telling herself she hated him…that he was a worthless cad, a two-timing player.

But what if she had been wrong? What if she had been terribly, dreadfully wrong?

He used his thumb to erase the frown lines between her brows. "What's the matter, buttercup?"

Hearing the silly nickname made the lump in her throat grow larger. "I don't know what we're doing, Jeff."

His smile was lopsided, more rueful than happy. "Damned if I know either. But let's worry about that tomorrow."

She cupped his cheek, feeling the light stubble of late-day beard. "Since when do *you* channel Scarlett O'Hara?"

Without answering, he reached in his discarded pants for a condom and took care of business. Then he moved between her thighs. "Put your arms around my neck, Lucy. I want to feel you skin to skin."

Fifteen

Jeff tried to live an honorable life. He gave to charity, offered work to those who needed it, supported his local civic organizations and donated large sums of money to the church where he had been baptized as an infant.

But lying in Lucy's arms, on the brink of restaking a claim that had lain dormant for two years, he would have sold his soul to the devil if he could have frozen time.

Lucy's eyes were closed.

"Look at me," he commanded. "I want you to see my face when I take you."

Her breath came in short, sharp pants. She nodded, her eyelids fluttering upward as she obeyed.

Gently, he spread her thighs and positioned his aching flesh against the moist, pink lips of her sex. When he pushed inside, he was pretty sure he blacked out for a moment. *Two years. Two damn years.*

It was everything he remembered and more. The

fragrance of her silky skin. The sound of her soft, incoherent cries. His body and his soul would have recognized her even in the dark, anywhere in the world.

He felt her heart beating against his chest. Or maybe it was his heart. It was impossible to separate the two. Burying his face in the crook of her shoulder, he moved in her steadily, sucking in a sharp breath when she wrapped her legs around his waist, driving him deeper.

He thrust slowly at first, but all the willpower in the world couldn't stem the tide of his hunger. His body betrayed him, his desire cresting sharply in a release that left him almost insensate.

Lucy hadn't come. He knew that. But his embarrassment was blunted by the sheer euphoria of being with her again. He kissed her cheek. "I'm sorry, love." He touched her gently, intimately, stroking and teasing until she climaxed, too. Afterward, he held her close for long minutes.

But reality eventually intruded.

Lucy reclined on her elbow, head propped on her hand. "May I ask you a very personal question?"

Though his breathing was still far from steady, he nodded. "Anything."

Lucy reached out and smoothed a lock of his hair. Her gaze was troubled. "When was the last time you had sex?"

Here it was. The first test of their tenuous reconciliation. "You should know," he said quietly. "You were there."

She went white, her expression anguished, tears spilling from her eyes and rolling down her cheeks. "You're lying," she whispered.

Her accusation angered him. But he gathered her into

his arms and held her as she sobbed. Two years of grief and separation. Two years of lost happiness.

"I know you don't believe me, Lucy." He combed her hair with his fingers. "Maybe you never will. Don't cry so hard. You'll make yourself sick."

Perhaps they should have talked first. But his need for her had obliterated everything else. Now she was distraught, and he didn't know how to help her get to the truth. Was this going to be the only moment they had? If so, he wasn't prepared to let it end so soon.

Feeling her nude body against his healed the raw places inside him. She was his. He would fight. For however long it took. No matter what happened, he was never letting her go again.

Sixteen

Lucy's brain whirled in sickening circles. Jeff wanted her to believe he hadn't been with another woman since she walked out on him. He expected her to believe he had not cheated on her.

She should have been elated…relieved. Instead, she was shattered and confused and overwhelmed. Was she going to be one of those women who blindly accepted whatever her lover told her? Where was her pride? Her intuition? Her intellect?

Jeff was silent, but tense. She knew him well enough to realize that he was angry. Even so, the strong arms holding her close were her only anchors at a moment when everything she thought she knew was shattering into tiny fragments and swirling away.

At last, the storm of grief passed. She lay against him limp with emotional distress. Taking a deep breath, she tried to sit up. "We need to go back to Royal. Right now. I need to see you and Kirsten in the same room at the same time to hash this out."

Jeff moved up against the headboard. His jaw was tight, but he scooped her into his lap. "It can wait until tomorrow. We deserve this night together, Lucy. You and I. No one else. Even if you don't believe me."

With her cheek against his chest, she seesawed between hope and despair. Was it possible she hadn't lost him after all, or was she being a credulous fool? If she had placed more trust in what they had from the beginning, it might never have come to this. Was it too late to repair the damage and to reclaim the future that had almost been destroyed?

And what if Jeff *had* initiated the kiss with Kirsten? Could she forgive him and move on? Was what they had worth another chance? Would their relationship ever be the same?

She was deeply moved, unbearably regretful, and at the same time giddy with hope. Tipping back her head so she could see his face, she memorized his features. The heavy-lidded green eyes. The strong chin. The slightly crooked nose. The tiny scar below his left cheekbone.

He gazed down at her with a half-smile. "Are we good?"

"I'm not sure." She wanted to say more. She wanted to pour out her heart…to tell him about the endless months of despair and loneliness. But now was not the time to be sad. "Kiss me again," she whispered unsteadily. "So I know this isn't a dream."

Jeff leaned her over his arm and gave her what she asked for, warm and slow…soft and deep. With each fractured sigh on her part and every ragged groan from him, arousal shimmered and spread until every cell of her body pulsed wildly with wanting him. She grabbed handfuls of his hair, trying to drag him closer.

He winced and laughed. “Easy, darlin’. I don’t want to go bald just yet.”

His trademark humor was one of the things that had attracted her to him in the beginning. That and his broad-shouldered, lanky body.

Before she knew what was happening, he had levered her onto her back and was leaning over her, shaping the curves of her breasts with his fingertips. Her nipples were so sensitive, she could hardly stand for him to touch them.

“I need you inside me again,” she pleaded.

“Not yet.” His smile was feral. “Have patience, Lucy, love. We’ve got all night.”

Seventeen

Jeff wanted to worship her body and mark it as his and drive her insane with pleasure. It was a tall order for a man still wrung out from his own release. Not that he wasn't ready for another round. He was. He definitely was. His erection throbbed with a hunger that wouldn't be sated anytime soon.

But somehow he had to make Lucy understand.

When he tasted the tips of her breasts, circled the areolas with his tongue, she gasped and arched her back. He pressed her to the mattress and moved south, teasing her belly button before kissing his way down her hips and thighs and legs one at a time. He even spent a few crazy minutes playing with her toes, and this from a man who had never once entertained a foot fetish.

By this point, she was calling him names…pleading for more.

He laughed, but it was a hoarse laugh. He knew the

joke was on him. All his plans to demonstrate how high he could push her evaporated in the driving urge to fill her and erase the memory of every hour that had separated them.

His brain was so fuzzy he only remembered the new condom at the last minute. Once he was ready, he knelt and lifted one of Lucy's legs onto his shoulder. He paused—only a moment—to appreciate the sensual picture she made.

Everything about her was perfect…from the graceful arch of her neck to her narrow waist to the small mole just below her right breast.

He touched her deliberately, stroking the little spot that made her body weep for him. Even though he was gentle and almost lazy in his caress, Lucy climaxed wildly, her release beautiful and real and utterly impossible to resist. "God, I want you," he muttered.

When he thrust inside her, her orgasm hit another peak. The feel of her inner muscles fluttering against his sex drove him to the brink of control. He went still… chest heaving, hips moving restlessly despite his pause.

"Lucy?"

Her teeth dug into her bottom lip. "Yes?"

"I was furious with you for not trusting me. But I never stopped loving you."

"Oh, Jeff…" The look on her face told him she wasn't there yet. She still had doubts. He could wait, maybe. He wanted her to be absolutely sure. For now it was enough to feel…and to know…

Lucy was his.

He retreated and lifted her onto her knees, stuffing pillows beneath her. Her butt was the prettiest thing he'd ever seen, heart-shaped and full. Lucy had bemoaned the curves of her bottom on numerous occasions. Tonight, as he palmed it and squeezed it and steadied himself against it to enter her again with one firm push, he decided he could spend the rest of his life proving to her how perfect it was.

Leaning forward, he gathered her hair into a ponytail, securing it with his fist and using the grip to turn her head. “Look in the mirror, Lucy. This is us. This is real.”

Eighteen

Lucy hadn't even noticed that the dresser was conveniently situated across from the bed…and that the mirror faithfully reflected Jeff's sun-bronzed body and her own paler frame. The carnal image was indelibly imprinted on her brain. As long as she lived, she would never forget this moment.

She closed her eyes and bent her head. Jeff released her hair, letting it fall around her face. Behind her, his harsh breathing was audible. At last, he moved with a muffled shout, slamming into her again and again until he shuddered and moaned and slumped on top of her as they both collapsed onto the mattress.

Minutes later…maybe hours, so skewed was her sense of time, she stirred. In the interim, they had untangled their bodies. Jeff lay flat on his back, one arm flung across his eyes. She snuggled against him, draping her leg across his hairy thigh. "Are you alive?"

"Mmph..."

It wasn't much of a response, but it made her smile.

She danced her fingertips over his rib cage. At one time, he had been very ticklish.

His face scrunched up and he batted her hand away. "Five minutes," he begged, the words slurred. "That's all I need."

"Take your time," she teased. She rested her cheek against his chest, feeling so light with happiness it was a wonder she didn't float up to the ceiling. Maybe she was being naive. Maybe he would hurt her again. But at the moment, none of that seemed to matter.

"You never gave me a chance to explain two years ago," he muttered.

His statement dampened her euphoria. "Would it have mattered? I was desperately hurt and in shock. I'm not sure anything you said would have gotten through to me."

"I deserved a fair hearing, Lucy. We were in a committed relationship, but you were too stubborn to be reasonable."

His eyes were closed, so she couldn't see his expression. But his jaw was tight.

Was it all an act? Jeff playing up his innocence?

There was only one way to know for sure, even if the prospect curled her stomach. "Will you do me a favor?" she asked quietly.

Jeff yawned. "The way I feel right now, you could ask me for the moon and I'd call NASA to help me get it for you."

She reared up on one elbow and gaped. "Why, Jeff Hartley! That was the most romantic thing you've ever said to me."

And there it was again. *Doubt.* Many a woman had been swayed by pretty words.

He chuckled, holding her tightly against his side. “I’ve had two years to practice,” he said. “Prepare to be amazed. But let’s not get off track. What’s this big favor you need from me?”

“Will you go with me to Kirsten’s house?”

His entire body froze. “If it’s all the same to you, I’d rather not come anywhere near that woman.”

She kissed his bicep. “Please. I have to hear the truth. I know you want me to take you on faith, but I need something more concrete. I need you to understand my doubts, and I need your moral support.”

“Damn it. That’s what I get for promising you the moon.”

Nineteen

The following morning when Lucy woke up, she didn't know where she was. And then it all came back to her in a rush of memories from the night before. She and Jeff Hartley had done naughty things in this huge bed. Naughty, wonderful things.

During the night, he had insisted on holding her close as they slept, though in truth, sleep had been far down the list of their favorite activities. Actually, ranking right below mind-blowing sex were the strawberries and champagne they had ordered from room service at 3:00 a.m.

Jeff was still asleep. She studied him unashamedly, feeling her heart swell with hope and then contract with fear. Loving him once had nearly destroyed her. Could she let herself love him again?

She flinched in surprise when the naked man beneath the covers moved and spoke. "I am not a peep show for your private entertainment," he mumbled.

Reaching beneath the sheet, she took him in her hand. “Are you sure?”

What followed was a very pleasant start to their morning. When they were both rumpled and limp with satisfaction, she poked his arm. “Time to put on some clothes and check out. I want to get this over with.”

An hour later, they were on the highway, headed back to Royal. Lucy sat rigid in her seat, her hands clenched in her lap. Layers of dread filled her stomach with each passing mile.

When they reached the fringes of Royal proper, Jeff pulled off on the side of the road and turned to face her. “There’s something else I need to tell you.”

She blanched. “Oh?”

“Nothing bad,” he said hastily, correctly reading her state of mind. “I want you to know that I had my bank transfer twenty thousand dollars to Kenny’s account before you and I ever made it to Midland. I wanted you and me to be intimate, but only if you wanted it, too.”

Lucy shook her head. “Thank you for that.” But even as she said the words, she wondered if his generosity might be a ploy to win her trust…to play the knight in shining armor.

Of course, Jeff knew where Kirsten lived. The party where Jeff and Lucy first connected had been down the street from Kirsten’s house. When Jeff parked at the curb, Lucy took a deep breath. “This is it, I guess.”

Jeff was at her side as they made their way up the walk. Lucy rang the bell. Kirsten herself opened the door…and upon seeing Lucy and Jeff together, immediately turned the color of milk, her expression distraught. She didn’t invite them in. They stood in an awkward trio with the noonday sun beaming down.

Lucy squared her shoulders. “It’s been painful having you treat me so coldly these last two years, Kirsten. But I have to know the truth. If Jeff kissed you and you were seduced into responding, I need to hear you admit it."

Kirsten scowled. "What does the sainted Jeff Hartley have to say about the whole mess? I suppose he's told you what a bitch I am…what a terrible friend."

"Actually, he hasn't said much of anything. The man I knew two years ago wouldn't have cheated on me. But the only other explanation is that my best friend deliberately ruined my wedding."

Kirsten wrapped her arms around her waist, her expression hunted. "Why would I do that?"

"I don't know. But I've run out of scenarios, and I'm damned tired of wondering." Kirsten sneered. "Men are pigs. They want what they can't have. Jeff put the moves on me. He cheated on you."

Suddenly, the pain was as fresh as if the incident had happened yesterday. Seeing Kirsten in Jeff's arms had nearly killed Lucy. But now she had to take one of them on faith. Either her childhood friend or her lover.

She stared at Kirsten. "Did *he* cheat on me? Or did *you*?"

It was a standoff two years in the making. No matter what the answer turned out to be, Lucy lost someone she cared about, someone she loved.

Jeff remained silent during the long, dreadful seconds that elapsed. Time settled into slow motion…

At last, Kirsten's face crumpled. Her eyes flashed with a combination of guilt and anger. "If you'd had more faith in him, nothing I did would have mattered."

Lucy gasped, struck by the truth in the accusation. But her own behavior wasn't on trial at the moment. Shock paralyzed her, despite the part of her that must have accepted the truth somewhere deep down inside. "So it's true?" Lucy spared one glance at Jeff, but he was stone-faced.

Kirsten shrugged. "It's true. Your precious Jeff is innocent."

Lucy trembled. Knowing was one thing. Hearing it bluntly stated out loud was painful…and baffling. "Why, Kirsten? I have to know why?"

Kirsten was almost defiant now. "I was jealous. Ever since we were kids, things seemed so easy for you. When we came back from college and you hooked up with Jeff at the party, I was furious. I'd had my eye on him for a long time."

Lucy shook her head in disbelief. "You were so popular, Kirsten. I don't even know what you mean."

Kirsten shrugged. "I hoarded my resentment. Everything came to a head the night of your rehearsal dinner. I saw my chance and I took it. I kissed Jeff. Because I knew you were right outside the door. He had nothing to do with it."

"Oh, Kirsten. You were my best friend."

The other woman shook her head. "But not anymore." Quietly, Kirsten closed the door.

Twenty

Jeff took Lucy's arm and steered her back toward the car. "Give her time," he said. "The two of you may get beyond this."

Lucy stared at him. "How can you be so calm?"

He caressed her cheek, his eyes filled with warmth. "I have you back in my life again, Lucy. Nothing can hurt me now."

"Take me home with you, Jeff. Please."

They made the trip in silence. Her thoughts were in shambles. How had she been so wrong about so many things?

In Jeff's living room, she prowled. He leaned a shoulder against the doorframe, his gaze following her around the room. At last, he sighed. "Sometimes we have to put the past behind us, sweetheart. We have to choose to be happy and move on."

At last, Lucy stood in front of him, hands on her hips.

"I love you, too, Jeff. I'm sorry I didn't trust you…that I didn't trust us. Kirsten had been my friend since we were nine years old. When I saw her in your arms, it didn't make sense. So my default was to doubt you. And maybe to doubt myself, too, because I fell in love with you so quickly." She took a deep breath. "I adore you. I suppose I'll have to spend the rest of my life making this up to you."

He pulled her close and kissed her hard, making her heart skip several beats. "Nonsense. We're not going to talk about it again. Today is our new beginning."

Even in the midst of an almost miraculous second chance, Lucy fretted. "There's one more thing."

He scooped her into his arms and carried her to the sofa, sprawling with her in his arms. "Go ahead," he said, his tone resigned.

"I don't want people to gossip about us. Can we please keep this quiet? At least until after Christmas? That will give me time to go back to Austin and turn in my notice. I'll have to sell my condo if I'm coming back to run the farm. I'll convince Kenny to turn down the Samson Oil offer and stick around until the new year."

Jeff's eyes narrowed…giving him the look of a really pissed off cowboy. "No way," he said, his jaw thrust out. "We're getting married this week. I'm not stupid."

She petted his shirtfront. "Then go with me to Austin," she said urgently. "We'll have a quiet wedding at the courthouse. Just you and me. But nobody has to know. I want time for us to be us." She kissed his chin. "You understand, don't you?"

He moved her beneath him on the sofa, unzipping her black pants and toying with the lacy edge of her undies. "As long as you're in my bed every night, I'll do whatever you want, Lucy. But I won't wait to put my ring on your finger."

She linked her arms around his neck, drawing his head down so she could kiss him. "Whatever you say, cowboy. I'm all yours."

* * * * *

Don't miss a single installment of
TEXAS CATTLEMAN'S CLUB:
LIES AND LULLABIES

Baby secrets and a scheming sheikh rock Royal, Texas

COURTING THE COWBOY BOSS
by USA TODAY *bestselling author Janice Maynard*

LONE STAR HOLIDAY PROPOSAL
by USA TODAY *bestselling author Yvonne Lindsay*

NANNY MAKES THREE
by Cat Schield

THE DOCTOR'S BABY DARE
by USA TODAY *bestselling author Michelle Celmer*

THE SEAL'S SECRET HEIRS
by Kat Cantrell

A SURPRISE FOR THE SHEIKH
by Sarah M. Anderson

IN PURSUIT OF HIS WIFE
by Kristi Gold

A BRIDE FOR THE BOSS
by USA TODAY *bestselling author Maureen Child*

If you're on Twitter, tell us what you think of Harlequin Desire! #harlequindesire

COMING NEXT MONTH FROM

Available December 1, 2015

#2413 BANE

The Westmorelands • by Brenda Jackson

Rancher and military hero Bane Westmoreland is on a mission to reconnect with the one who got away—his estranged wife. And when the beautiful chemist's discovery puts her in danger, Bane vows to protect her at all costs...

#2414 TRIPLETS UNDER THE TREE

Billionaires and Babies • by Kat Cantrell

A plane crash took his memory. But then billionaire fighter Antonio Cavallari makes it home for the holidays only to discover the triplets he never knew...and their very off-limits, very tempting surrogate mother.

#2415 LONE STAR HOLIDAY PROPOSAL

Texas Cattleman's Club: Lies and Lullabies

by Yvonne Lindsay

At risk of losing her business, single mother Raina Patterson finds solace in the arms of Texas deal-maker Nolan Dane. But does this mysterious stranger have a hidden agenda that will put her heart at even bigger risk?

#2416 A WHITE WEDDING CHRISTMAS

Brides and Belles • by Andrea Laurence

When a cynical wedding planner is forced to work with her teenage crush to plan his sister's Christmas wedding, sparks fly! But will she finally find a happily-ever-after of her own with this second-chance man?

#2417 THE RANCHER'S SECRET SON

Lone Star Legends • by Sara Orwig

For wealthy rancher Nick Milan, hearing the woman he loved and lost tell him he's a daddy is the shock of a lifetime. The revelation could derail his political career...or put the real prize back within tantalizing reach...

#2418 TAKING THE BOSS TO BED

by Joss Wood

After producer Ryan Jackson kisses a stranger to save her from his client's unwanted attentions, he realizes she's actually his newest employee! Faking a relationship is now essential for business, but soon real passion becomes the bottom line...

SPECIAL EXCERPT FROM

HARLEQUIN® Desire

Bane Westmoreland and Crystal Newsome secretly eloped when they were young—but then their families tore them apart. Now, five years later, Bane is coming back for his woman, and no one will stop him.

Read on for a sneak peek of BANE
the final book in Brenda Jackson*'s*
***THE WESTMORELAND** series*

With her heart thundering hard in her chest, Crystal began throwing items in the suitcase open on her bed. Had she imagined it or had she been watched when she'd entered her home tonight? She had glanced around several times and hadn't noticed anything or anyone. But still…

She took a deep breath, knowing she couldn't lose her cool. She made a decision to leave her car here and a few lights burning inside her house to give the impression she was home. She would call a cab to take her to the airport and would take only the necessities and a few items of clothing. She could buy anything else she needed.

But this, she thought as she studied the photo album she held in her hand, went everywhere with her. She had purchased it right after her last phone call with Bane. Her parents had sent Crystal to live with Aunt Rachel to finish out the last year of school. They wanted to get her away from Bane, not knowing she and Bane had secretly married.

A couple of months after she left Denver, she'd gotten a call from him. He'd told her he'd enlisted in the navy because he needed to grow up, become responsible and make something out of himself. She deserved a man who could be all that he could be, and after he'd accomplished that goal he would come for her. Sitting on the edge of the bed now, she flipped through the album, which she had dedicated to Bane. She thought of him often. Every day. What she tried not to think about was why it was taking him so long to come back for her, or how he might be somewhere enjoying life without her. Forcing those thoughts from her mind, she packed the album in her luggage.

Moments later, she had rolled her luggage into the living room and was calling for a cab when her doorbell rang.

She went still. Nobody ever visited her. Who would be doing so now? She crept back into the shadows of her hallway, hoping whoever was at the door would think she wasn't home. She held her breath when the doorbell sounded again. Did the person on the other side know she was there?

She rushed into her bedroom and grabbed her revolver out of the nightstand drawer. By the time she'd made it back to the living room, there was a second knock. She moved toward the door, but stopped five feet away. "Who is it?" She tightened her hands on the revolver.

There was a moment of silence. And then a voice said, "It's me, Crystal. Bane."

Bane will do whatever it takes to keep his woman safe, but will it be enough?